Tend My Flowers

CATHLEEN ELLIS

Cover design by Launie Parry
Interior design by Veronica Yager

ISBN: 978-1-62967-088-1
Library of Congress Control Number: 2017901438

OTHER BOOKS BY CATHLEEN ELLIS

www.CathleenEllis.com

A Scarf of Promise

Castle in the Air

Making Our Way

Kara's Love

Baskets on Christmas Lane

Up To Me

Christmas Bright

A Voice for Gabby

Love Ties

Roses for Meredith

Old Crooked Road

Just Let It Go

1

"Mom, I'm here," Lindsey spoke up after she walked into the shop. She took a deep breath and absorbed the flower smells, the roses and carnations, her favorites.

"In the back, by the delivery door."

"Hey, I had a good day," Lindsey O'Ranon smiled to her mom as they moved closer together.

Mariah hugged her daughter, "I'm glad your day was good, yup, behind, as always for this time of year."

As her mom stepped back from her, Lindsey watched a big smile spread across her mom's face.

"I've decided, babe. I'm going to let you study for your GED."

Mariah watched the look on her daughter's face, eyebrows raised and forehead creased, eyes wide open. Lindsey stood there, her mouth agape. Just then the phone rang. Lindsey automatically picked it up. The long distance order took her some time to fill.

"Yes, ma'am, that order will be delivered tomorrow by 3 p.m. Yes, Happy Holidays to you too."

Lindsey logged in the order information for tomorrow's calendar on the computer.

"Is Lily on deliveries?"

"Uh huh, we've had a bunch. It's been a great month in the shop; with Christmas on a Saturday, we'll have a whole week for sales, last minute stuff, which you saw happen last year."

Mother and daughter stood together at the work table, in plain view of the front door so they could assist customers when they arrived. The two women prepared flower arrangements for tomorrow's deliveries. They dropped stems of flowers, discarded flowers, and damaged greenery to the messy floor.

"Mom, what made you change your mind, what happened, you and me, we been fightin' over school 'most all this semester, and whew," Lindsey paused and exhaled a big breathe, "all last year?"

"Honey, I've decided you're right about all this. You are smart; you do it all in the shop except the tech stuff that we leave for our computer guys. You handle the bookkeeping; you're taking it in school, the only class you like."

"Yeah, it is; I just don't care about the rest of my classes, uh, I guess science classes were OK. Mom, I hate school, it's sssooo boring." Lindsey paused and looked into her mom's eyes, "I am a real smart ass attitude-wise at school, but the classroom, isn't like the real world. Right here in this shop, Mom, this is the real world, the math and technology parts, the people skills parts, making a profit, like you have to do, to survive. Us kids in high school, we take and take, not worrying about surviving like you parents do."

Lindsey stopped and breathed in, "Uuummm, so, I bought the books to prepare for the ACT and SAT, if I ever decide college is something I need to do. I'll study the test prep books, plus attend GED prep at night. Hey, you know how well I did on my PSAT; I'm still learnin' stuff."

"Lindsey, your scores on your PSAT put you in contention for a National Merit Scholarship. Your counselor called me to tell me that. But that's not what you're looking for right now. You're not having a senior year of high school."

Mariah gazed at her daughter, pretty, smart, helpful, but knowing her own mind.

"Yeah, Mom, I gotta face it, I don't have a prayer making it as a National Merit Scholarship finalist. Just take a look at my record, grades aren't great, I don't have extracurricular activities, just track, my teachers didn't care for my attitude, I'm just not scholarship material. I won't even graduate from high school." She stopped and smiled to her mom, "I test well and, yes, I am smart."

"You are certainly that, and Lindsey, you'll get your GED by the end of spring semester?"

"I promise, that's my plan, I told you I'm already signed up, start right away in January. I'll work in the shop days, study here when I can, then class at night. Mom, this is what I want to do; God agrees."

Mariah nodded her acknowledgement of what Lindsey just said, "And finals?"

"I'm done Tuesday, the twenty-first," Lindsey blew out a big breath, "way done with high school."

Studying for your driver's license test?"

"I am."

"Girl, you got plenty going on."

Lindsey held her mom's shoulder, "I love Christmas, the bestest, wonderfulest time of the year."

"My bestest present, seeing a shine in your eyes, and a happy note to your voice, Lindsey, you been unhappy for a while," Mariah caught her daughter's eyes with hers and smiled.

"Mom," Mariah watched Lindsey's eyes tear up, "wanted to tell you, now's the time," she nodded and paused for a minute, "I loved him. Rocky, well he got his way, and then he dumped me." Lindsey stopped, swallowed hard and went on, "I know it's best, leave school with a clean break. I really really liked him, thought I loved him, but he wasn't a friend. I never really said anything to him about my plans. Geez, I am way past high school, it's unbelievable. He's still so high school, hopin' every chick will be his. Mom, I gotta get used to disappointment. He was a big one for me. But I'll go on, anyway."

Mariah turned to her daughter, "Sounds like you're clearing your plate for your future."

"I am, Mom," Lindsey nodded to her, "we're almost finished here; is Uncle Caleb making dinner tonight?"

"Yeah, it's his night."

Within 20 minutes the shop came to order for the next day, as they nestled the holiday arrangements in the big walk-in coolers for delivery in the morning, swept the floor and cleared counters.

Then Lindsey heard the familiar refrain as her mom dead bolted the front door, "All right, shop, tend my flowers."

Ever since Lindsey helped close the shop her mom always said that as they left. It brought a smile to Lindsey's lips, her mom's shop. She was the caretaker of flowers.

§O

The three of them held hands as Mariah said grace. At Amen, they squeezed hands and let go.

"Uuummm, the spaghetti is delish, Uncle Caleb," Lindsey complimented him as she shook more Parmesan cheese onto her spaghetti. They downed almost a whole loaf of French bread, which Caleb cut up into slices covered with melted butter and his rendition of a garlic spread.

Mariah looked from her daughter to her brother.

"Bro, it's nice to see you smile. How was PT, and your visit to the chaplain?"

"Good, good, ever day, a little better, I even worked a half day at the Senior Center."

Mariah invited her brother, a wounded warrior, to stay with them after his medical release from the military. He contributed his share of the rent and helped buy groceries. Mariah and Lindsey lived in a rental home for two years now. Before that they had a nice home, but that got lost in the divorce settlement Lindsey's dad had with Mariah. Joe O'Ranon wanted out of the marriage after he walked away from his family. His lawyer got him half of everything.

Lindsey recalled Mariah returning again and again to another saying of hers, "God don't make no mistakes, while we sleep, He's awake."

Lindsey watched her mom throughout dinner, "She's a super smart lady, has such a good business sense, she loves her shop, and the flowers. She's livin' her dream. I will be so happy to work with her more hours, to make her dream a success, hey she's already doing successful," Lindsey thought.

Mariah made plans for the next year. Lily was Mariah's helper since she bought The Flower Shop on Main Street in Porttown, Iowa two years ago. The business brought in enough sales to keep Lily on and bring Lindsey on full time. Mariah had a line of credit with a local bank to assist her with cash flow problems during the quiet months when the flower shop's profits dropped.

Sleep started to take Lindsey that Friday night as she felt comforted with her mom's letting her get the GED.

"There will be men in my life, guys to love, to care for, guys who'll be interested in my future, guys who'll want the best for me. I fell to lust and learned one hell of a lesson," she spoke out as she looked at the stars shining out her bedroom window.

ഇ

"Lily, you'll deliver twice today, right?" Mariah asked as Lily and Lindsey stood with her at the work table on Saturday morning.

Lily nodded as she left with deliveries. The phone rang a lot; Lindsey answered and Mariah kept filling orders. At 9:30 Mariah pulled off her apron.

"I want like crazy to spend time with my friend, Jude, who's in town just for today."

"Mom, get outa here; meet your friend. We'll be fine, things'll settle down."

Mariah washed up and hurried up to the counter. She gave Lindsey a hug and an "I love you."

"Back atsha, Mom," Lindsey smiled to her mom and nodded as she picked up the ringing phone.

Lindsey watched her mom turn around at the door and blow her a kiss. Lindsey waved with her free hand. While Lindsey filled orders for the afternoon deliveries, she talked out the next few days of activities. "Tomorrow, study for finals, just a little bit. Monday and Tuesday, take finals, and high school's out forever for me. Wednesday, my birthday, get my license, help in the shop on Thursday and Friday. Wow, Christmas Saturday, a whole week of business in the shop before Christmas; Mom's doing great this holiday season. And I'm so happy."

Lindsey smiled to herself as she looked around the shop. She moved back to the cooler and brought out the bunches of flowers she needed. Lily was out on her deliveries. Lindsey had her hands full of flowers as she looked to the front of the shop. Two men in uniforms approached her.

"Happy Holidays, officers, what can this shop girl help you with?" She gave them a big smile, "A special bouquet for a loved one?"

The officers did not smile back to her. She knew Officer Linnon because of the Girl Scout group his daughter and Lindsey were in a few years ago. Lindsey set her flowers down on the work table and looked back at them.

"Lindsey, can we sit down with you at the table where you talk to customers about what they need?"

"Of course, you must have a very special order in mind," Lindsey concluded.

"Your mom, Lindsey."

Lindsey nodded, "She took time off to have a special lunch with a friend."

"There's been an accident."

"An accident?"

Lindsey tried to concentrate on those two words as she sat down with them.

"Your mom and the other driver, head on."

"They're gone?"

"Other driver instantly, your mom without brain activity, after donating her organs, your Uncle Caleb, uh, we are so sorry. Your Uncle Caleb is on the way from the hospital."

Lindsey got up, walked up and down the shop again and again, holding her hands together in a tight grip. She kept walking, and then she abruptly sat down with the officers. Her uncle walked into the shop, coming slowly to the three of them seated. Lindsey watched him, noting his slight limp, his physical therapy really helped.

Lindsey got up and went to him.

She looked up into his eyes, "Uncle Caleb, is it just us?"

Caleb's tears began as they hugged.

"Honey bear, it's us, God's with us, the three of us will do this; you are strong, stronger than you know."

Lindsey sat down. She cried just a little after she put her head down. She raised up.

"Officers, I'm in shock. I can't wrap my mind around this. But I got a business to run and," she looked around at the clock, "there's a little time left."

Caleb sat with the officers as Lindsey got up and put her shop brain on. From time to time she let lose with quiet tears. Lily returned and took over the phone and an incoming customer as she began to understand the news. Lindsey stepped to the back and knelt down by the desk. She put one hand on the desk to support herself as she wavered side to side.

"God's will, right God?" Lindsey sobbed for several minutes. She cleared her throat and whispered, "God, help us."

She returned to the three men seated at the table. Caleb took notes and stood with the officers after they finished. They all shook hands.

"Caleb and Lindsey, we are so sorry for your loss," Officer Linnon spoke for both men as they were leaving.

"Lindsey, what can I do to help?"

Lindsey looked up to Caleb and gave him a tiny smile, "You deal with everything for mom. There needs to be a funeral, right?"

"Roger that, and Lindsey, when I got the phone call from the police, I asked them to alert the hospital that Mariah's an organ donor, that organs should be harvested."

Tears filled Lindsey's eyes, "Uh, Uncle Caleb, I don't know what that means."

"Ah, right, her organs that can be," he nodded his head to her, "will go to organ donations. I signed the papers at the hospital before I came here."

"Oh wow, that means she'll live on through other people, right?"

"Uh huh, she may be able to give others life through donating, like her kidneys, or her heart, or her eyes, she had 20-20 vision."

Lindsey paused, "That's wonderful, Uncle Caleb, how did you know about all that?"

She watched as his eyes hooded, "The war, Lindsey."

In slow motion she moved and stood in front of Caleb.

"The legal stuff; Mom's filled me in about a lot of it since I already do the books. But I'm not of age to help until Wednesday."

"Hug?"

Lindsey nodded, hugging Caleb. Lily joined in the group hug. They cried together for several minutes and then let go of each other. Tissues went all around as a customer came into the shop. Lindsey didn't know how, but they got through that last hour in the shop.

"Next week's critical, one of our busiest of the year," Lindsey paused as she looked at Caleb and Lily, "people want flowers sent, they decide at the last minute. Look in the coolers; we got a lot to deliver Monday morning to customers, and three flower orders coming in through the week. We gotta keep this business open; it's what mom wants. I can't see her any more, but she's in my memory and in my heart."

Caleb and Lily nodded to her, "Yes, you're right. We go on."

ℰꙩ

The home phone rang a lot late Saturday afternoon and early evening. Caleb answered the calls and took charge after he and Lindsey did quick lists of what needed to be accomplished.

Mariah made no attempt to keep house, being at the shop all the time. Lindsey kept her own room and the two bathrooms neat and clean. The rest of the home did not meet Lindsey's housekeeping standards. She kept her mouth shut through the years about that. Now she acted; FREAKIN' DECLUTTER was first on her list. Within an hour she and her trash bags worked their way from the front living room through the combination kitchen and dining area, back through the guest bedroom/computer room/study. Her uncle's room was his business, but he kept it Army neat, organized. When Caleb was not on the phone, she vacuumed. In her mother's room she made the bed, straightened the room and hung up her mom's clothes. She found her mother's personal notebook where Mariah kept a copy of her will and her lawyer's name and phone number, checkbook and savings account book, safety deposit box key, life and car insurance policies, divorce decree, credit card information, car title, rental agreement on the house they lived in, and instructions for everything Mariah thought Lindsey must know. Mariah and Lindsey went through the notebook earlier in the year. At that time Mariah added Lindsey as a signer on her checkbook and savings accounts as well as the safety deposit box, to be effective when Lindsey turned 16.

Lindsey also got her own checking account where she deposited the checks for the work she did at the shop. She was a part-time employee. Lindsey's mother designated her as the beneficiary on her life insurance policy. Mariah showed her the copy of the beneficiary form that was with the policy.

Lindsey recalled, "Babe, if anything ever happens to me," then she remembered her mom's smile and the shake of her head, "well, the life insurance monies will help you pay off the bank loan on the shop and shop van and leave you money that I suggest you stash away for your college education. Your dad's been good about paying me child support for you. Every month I get a check; it helps with rent and groceries, that's the agreement 'til you're 18."

Lindsey remembered her own reply, "No way, Mom, I don't think college is for me."

Tears welled up in Lindsey's eyes. She just let the sadness wash over her, again and again. All of a sudden she understood; her mom did want her to go to college someday. After a few minutes, Lindsey's tears subsided as she felt a hand on her shoulder.

"What can I do to help you, Lindsey?" Uncle Caleb asked her as he stood to her side as she sat on her mom's bed.

"Nahda, just gotta let the pain happen."

"Are you about finished with the cleaning?"

Lindsey rose from the bed and put her mother's notebook back in its place in the closet.

"Yeah, just gotta vacuum her bedroom. Hey, I'm hungry. Can we order pizza please?"

"Jen called; she's coming over, I'll order enough pizza for the three of us, OK?"

Lindsey nodded to her uncle and gathered the trash she collected throughout the house. She took the trash bags and set them by the door out to the garage. After she put away the vacuum, she added the bags to the trash containers in the garage. She looked around the garage and opened the door back into the house.

"Hey, Uncle Caleb, can you please come out to the garage?"

"What?"

"Remember how you always complain about having to scrape your windshield on cold mornings?"

"Uh huh."

"Dude, get your car key, I'm opening the garage door and I want you to put your pickup in here. I'll move stuff over, so you'll have plenty of room. Gosh, it's a two-car garage, but you wouldn't know it for all the stuff."

Lindsey moved things around and soon Caleb had his wheels inside.

"Caleb," she began to cry, "we got to get a lot of stuff to the thrift stores. I'll not have junk around. People need this stuff. You'll help me, once things settle down, right?"

He came up to her and looked down into her eyes, "Honey bear, I'll help you any way I can."

℥

"Lindsey, I'm so sorry, let me know what I can do to help you get through this," Jen said after she and Lindsey hugged.

Jen remained Lindsey's best friend throughout the years. They were a study in contrasts. Jen stood 5'8", with black curly hair and brown eyes. Lindsey's tallest stretch made her 5'2", with blonde hair curling below her shoulders and sea green eyes. Jen loved school, made mostly A's, and prided herself on her plan to attend college and go on to medical school. Lindsey got by with B's and an occasional A, took a lot of science classes, but remained unmotivated except in the business courses she took. She completely understood why her teachers disliked her attitude about school. Lindsey knew she was smart. Her teachers admonished her for her lack of motivation to study.

Lindsey and Jen sat on the carpet in front of the sparking fire. They pulled up a recliner so Caleb could stretch out his below-the-knee prosthetic leg and still enjoy the fire. They downed piece after piece of the combo pizza: pepperoni, sausage, Canadian bacon, olives and green peppers. The teens washed their food down with pop, and Caleb drank a beer.

"Rude to ask, also none of my business, but, guys, the plans for your sis, your mom?" Jen asked as she looked from Caleb to Lindsey.

"Yeah, Jen, we're making headway. Funeral's Tuesday morning at 10:30 at Our Redeemer United Methodist; Mariah's being cremated, it's what the mortician said was best," his voice began wavering and he paused, "given that there were donations of her organs. There'll be a luncheon in the church fellowship hall at 11:30. Those church women are so wonderful, to do this right before Christmas. We help with that expense. Reverend Tompkins, he's one of a kind, to get this all put together on such short notice." Caleb paused and smiled to them, "he's coming over later this evening."

"Good, Uncle Caleb, I've decided, I'll ask Lily to keep the shop open and just close up for an hour so she can attend the luncheon on Tuesday. She told me she did not want to go to the funeral. Then we'll head back to work."

"I'll be at the funeral, or the luncheon, depending on how long my finals take, on Tuesday morning, OK, Lindsey?

Lindsey nodded her head and hugged her friend.

℘

Sunday morning dawned cold and frosty. Lindsey left her home early enough for her to walk to church.

"I wish I could run, but it's icy some places; I need to let go of the sadness, the pain, I'll just hustle along," she spoke out as her small body picked up the pace.

Lindsey slipped into a back pew as the service started. She kept bringing her mind back to the singing and Reverend Tompkin's message. On that Sunday before Christmas he spoke about the light of love, that love helps restore every lost voice.

"I'm so glad Reverend came to see me and Caleb last evening. I'll see him for grief counseling, I know I need to go 'cause right now I feel like one of those lost voices," she pondered that as she got up for the final prayer.

Lindsey left the church just as the service ended. She abhorred any attention; she wanted to be alone. The tears came as she walked back home at a slower pace. She looked up into the gray Iowa sky. She remembered now; the sun, it had not shown since Friday afternoon.

"That fits," Lindsey spoke out, "God is sad to lose mom to the earth, but glad to take her to heaven to be with Him. Soon He'll bring back the sun."

ဆာ

Caleb handled the home phone all the rest of the day Sunday. Several neighbors and friends of Mariah's stopped by with cupcakes, casseroles, an apple pie, and words of encouragement. Lindsey sat on the floor in her bedroom. Her school books lay around her. She studied as much as she felt it would do her any good. Then she decided.

"Uncle Caleb, I'm gonna ask if I can take all my finals tomorrow. I just have two on Tuesday; I tell ya, high school is such a friggin' waste of my time."

Caleb saw the disgusted look on his niece's face, her eyes gray with sadness, not their usual calm green.

"Under the circumstances, I'd say that is a good request. Lily and I'll handle the shop until you're done Monday."

"I'm hoping I'll be at the shop by 2:30. This is a monster week for us; oh how I love the last-minute folks, mostly guys, who realize, finally, what's happening, duh, hey dude, it's Christmas."

Caleb saw a tiny smile on Lindsey's face as a giggle escaped her lips.

"Hey, you're taking me for our appointment for my driver's test on Wednesday, right?"

"Yeah, you've driven my pickup; it's all we got, Lindsey."

"Right, I don't think my driving examiner would appreciate being hauled around in a flower delivery van."

"Not."

Lindsey watched as he shook his head.

ℰℂ

"Thank goodness for notebooks," Lindsey said to her uncle as she removed them from the office shelf.

She completed her finals; all of her teachers expressed their sorrow at the loss of her mom. It was 3:30 p.m. Monday. Lindsey closed the door on her high school years.

Lily went out on deliveries. The phone sat quiet for a brief time. Lindsey pointed out information that Caleb needed to read. Mariah broke down the shop operations by day, week, month and year in a notebook.

"Wow, Lindsey, your mom, holy cow, super organized, she laid it all out here, looks like we've got all the dates of when taxes and everything's due. It looks complicated, but we'll take it one day at a time."

"Right, Uncle Caleb, I been through the whole shop process for a couple of years. It'll all work out, and mom's CPA will help us. I've already talked to him," she nodded to her uncle.

Lindsey stood, working on her next floral project.

"Lindsey," Caleb spoke.

"Yeah?"

"Your mom put me on as a signer for the shop business checks; she did that soon after I got here. You've had me sign a few checks instead of her. You never asked."

"Never thought about it, mom just said there needed to be another person able to sign the checks; she was thinking of the future, that's my mom."

The phone rang. Lindsey wrote out the information.

"I've got the order, yes, the wreath will be at the front, near the cremains. Thank you very much for your call."

Lindsey logged in the request and set to work.

"It's lucky we made several extra wreaths; certainly didn't expect one for the funeral. Uncle Caleb, could I talk to you?"

Caleb stepped out of the big cooler. A flower order for the shop came in earlier, and he just finished loading everything into the cooler.

"Never gonna believe the request I just took," she shook her head to him.

He watched her as tears formed in her eyes.

"It's from a florist where your sister, Crystal, and Grandma live."

"Wow, I haven't heard from Crystal for a very long time; mom, your grandma, is so far gone, Mariah and I just stopped checking on her. Neither mom nor Crystal wanted to have anything to do with us, for like forever," Caleb spoke in a soft tone. "I wonder how they heard about Mariah's death."

Lindsey brought out a wreath from the middle cooler. She wiped away her tears.

"Well, your sister's done this order. Here's what I'm supposed to write on the card, 'Dear Lindsey and Caleb, Can't come for Mariah's funeral; do know that you are in our thoughts and prayers. Love, Crystal and Mom/Grandma'"

Caleb came up to Lindsey and hugged her.

"Geez, Uncle Caleb, was she even aware that mom owned this flower shop in Porttown?"

"I dunno, since mom's dementia took hold of her, and of Crystal, I suspect maybe Crystal didn't realize what Mariah's been doing. For whatever reason, they both dislike us, me and Mariah. Think this is a really positive step, a reaching out which hasn't happened before."

"Something good to come out of mom's death?"

"Uh huh, we'll see."

Caleb saw the hopeful look on Lindsey's face and realized the tone of his voice was all wrong.

"Sorry," he paused, "I sound pessimistic; it's just that we've, your mom and me, had a really rough go of it with your Aunt Crystal and Grandma. I mentioned a positive step, that's what this is."

"Sounds like Grandma's dementia put a choke hold on mom's family. Mom never spoke about Crystal or Grandma. I am so glad you live with us.

I mean, now with me. I need a guardian; you'll be that, won't you?"

"I will Lindsey; I'm committed to help you with the shop so you can get your GED and decide about a possible future education for yourself."

"Uncle Caleb, we gotta take it easy, one day at a time; I'm still not focusing on mom being gone. I don't know when I'll realize it. I just let the sadness take me now."

Caleb nodded his head to her as she began decorating the wreath for their mom.

"Uncle Caleb," she asked, as she turned to him, "will you promise me that you will keep up with your recovery efforts, especially the emotional stuff. It's important to me that you get to the point where you will get training for a job down the road."

Caleb touched her upper arm, "I promise, Lindsey."

℘

"I'm making another pot of coffee, Lindsey, do you want some?"

"Maybe I'll try it; I know mom drank coffee at work, had a pot there. Uncle Caleb, show me where stuff is kept; I can make it for us, might be a good thing for me to learn how to do."

Lindsey checked the time; they needed to be at the church by 10:05. Caleb and Lindsey delivered a floral arrangement and the wreath to the church altar earlier that morning.

"I'd like some, Lindsey, please."

Her dad held up his cup so she could pour him coffee.

After her mom died she called her dad. He asked what he could do to help, and she asked him to come to the funeral. Now here they were, the three of them sat at the dining room table, drinking coffee and eating cinnamon rolls Lindsey baked earlier.

"Thanks for coming, Dad."

Lindsey watched her dad's eyes, tears glistening in them.

"I never stopped loving her," he paused and nodded, "your mom. Our differences just grew, as you grew up, Lindsey. It was in sheer frustration that I walked out on the two of you. I thank you so much for letting me stay here last night. It helped me catch up on your life."

"I'll write you, Dad, haven't done that much, and I should have. I had a lot of anger, but that did me no good, fer sure. And sorry about the dirty sheets; thanks for washing them. Uh, mom did the wash only when it piled sky high. So I started washing all my own stuff years ago."

Lindsey's dad smiled to her, "And I can call you, unbelievable that you're going for your GED, young lady, in a year, or as soon as you want to, you could go on and further your education. Your mom always wanted that for you." He paused, "And me also," he nodded to her.

"Dad, for right now and until I decide different, The Flower Shop is my life, my mom's dream, but my dream now." She nodded her head as she watched her dad's eyes, "And I know that can change, change quick, just look at what's happened in just a few days, Uncle Caleb's gonna help, and I'll keep Lily on. Stuff will settle down. And I must learn patience. That was seriously my problem with school; I jumped ahead, had my books all read, hated waiting for my teachers to explain stuff; it just took too long. I hope, Uncle Caleb, as I've already mentioned, that you'll decide to pursue training of some kind or go for a degree."

Lindsey noticed Caleb's nod, "I will, I just don't know what yet. Right now," he grinned to her, "it's runnin' a business with you, Lindsey."

℘

"Uncle Caleb, you look super great in your uniform and beret. If mom is looking down on us, she'll be so pleased."

Lindsey looked up to him as she made her remark.

"Honey bear, are you ready?"

"Uh huh, I'm glad we sent dad on ahead."

Lindsey held Caleb's arm. They walked at a slow pace down the aisle as they turned from side to side to greet people they knew. Several of her teachers, one her track coach, nodded as she passed by in her black outfit. For some folks, this was the first time they saw Caleb. He dressed in his service greens. Today he limped a little more, from a lot of time spent on his feet in the flower shop. Reverend Tompkin kept the service to a half hour, a celebration of Mariah's life. Caleb introduced himself to the congregation and spoke for a short time, and Lindsey read a piece she said comforted her.

"Perhaps they are not the stars, but rather openings in heaven where the love of our lost one pours through and shines down upon us," she looked up and scanned the congregation, "to let us know she is happy and at peace in a place filled with love."

One of the young choir members, a teen in Lindsey's junior class, sang the only song at the end of the service. *Be Still My Soul* rang out through the church's assemblage. What Lindsey heard as the hymn concluded were the words, "When change and tears are past....blessed we shall meet at last."

"It's finally starting to sink in, mom is really gone," she spoke out as the tears streamed down her face.

The luncheon followed in the church's fellowship hall. Everyone ate and talked. Lindsey tried to stop at every table to say hello and to thank folks for coming during this busy holiday time. Caleb did the same thing. He received polite inquiries about his military service. Many folks thanked him for what he did in the military. Lindsey did not realize until now that Mariah was the president of the Business Owners Association of Porttown. Her mom wore several hats in her business dealings.

As she hurried to leave, she paused in the kitchen, thanking the Women's Circle for putting together the delicious luncheon of sandwiches, veggie trays, and three mouthwatering desserts.

Lindsey put a brave smile on and waved, "I got a business to run. You'll send us the bill for this, right, to the shop? I mean this, Happy Holidays to all of you, we go on."

The church member in charge nodded. The women standing there waved to her. Lindsey saw tears in many of their eyes. She felt a lightness that came from her heart, a lot of folks cared.

℅

Lily walked out of the big cooler with flowers in her arms.

"Thanks for coming back and opening up the shop, Lily."

"I got a chance to eat and chat with folks. Your mom, she sure was well liked." Lily paused, "Man, there's a lot to do," she nodded to Caleb and Lindsey as they came to the back of the shop with Mariah's memorial wreath.

Lindsey carried a large envelope. Reverend asked them to keep the wreath. They donated the other flower arrangement back to the mortuary for a funeral service the next day at the mortuary. Mariah's cremains also went back to the mortuary for safe keeping until Caleb and Lindsey decided about a location for interment.

"We're going to put this wreath on our front door at home. It'll look great until at least Valentine's Day."

"Good idea, guys," Lily smiled to them.

After she put on her apron over the outfit she wore to the funeral, Lindsey grabbed a paper and printed: thank you's, decide where to bury mom's cremains, write dad, cancel mom's car insurance, for starters. She scotch taped the paper where she would find it on her way out, on her small purse. Lindsey kept a large envelope right below her purse. The packet contained her mom's death certificates, 20 of them.

2

"I'm licensed, Uncle Caleb, thank you so much for waiting for me," Lindsey said.

Caleb watched her smile widen and her eyes brighten as she showed him her license.

"Good job, honey bear, hey nice picture, that didn't take as long as I expected."

"Nah, not many people want to come in Christmas week. They got other stuff going on. My driving examiner sure was nice; she knew mom and told me how sorry she was to hear what happened. I just about lost it. And of course I aced my written exam."

"When do you want to start driving the shop van?"

"Maybe in a day or two, hey mom let me drive it for deliveries when I had my permit. But I wasn't alone. This'll be different."

Caleb let her drive his pickup back to the shop. Lily spoke on the phone, and a customer waited for her to finish. Lindsey took over with the customer and got his information for filling the order. By the end of the day Lindsey felt achy in every bone of her body. She checked in with Lily.

"Sweetie, stretch out, try to relax, do some of those exercises you told me about. Remember, you been through an emotional hell, a shock that's still takin' hold of you, your mind, and now, your body."

They closed the shop.

"A couple more days, so far this is our best Christmas," Lily smiled to them as she got ready to leave.

"Uncle Caleb, you drive home; please take the wreath. I want to stay on in the shop by myself for just a little and talk to mom. It's just four blocks; I'll bring the death certificates."

SO

Lindsey looked around the orderly shop, the floors and countertops clean. She stood up tall and straight, feeling proud of the lovely holiday accessories scattered throughout the shop.

"OK Mom, it's the end of day two in the shop without you, remember Saturday you were here with us for a little while. I know you're lookin' down, proud of our efforts. We'll do this, we can, we haf to. I love you," Lindsey paused, and spoke out again, "my brain fog goes away, a little bit at a time."

As she approached the front door of their home, Lindsey saw that her uncle already placed the wreath there. When she got inside, she took her purse, coat and packet back to her bedroom.

"I'm not hungry, Lindsey, I'm going out for a little while, need to clear my head, you'll be OK?" he asked.

"Of course, you've been house bound and shop bound for a long time now. You need to get out."

"Anything you need?"

"Let's talk about it tomorrow morning, but Uncle Caleb, I've seen a lot of shows on cable. One of the things that seem to happen a lot, on the romance shows especially, when someone dies, is that the bank calls in the loan the dead person had. I always thought that was so damn cruel. But I think that could happen to us. I'm scared about that."

Lindsey searched her uncle's face; he saw her distress in her squinty eyes and grim lips.

"It's a local bank, but they want their money. I feel certain they'll think we can't make it now that mom's gone. And I understand," she swallowed hard, "they just don't want to take the risk. I just hope the bank gives me enough time to get them the money on the loan. I need to make it clear to the bank that we'll continue to make this shop profitable. We've called mom's life insurance company. Tomorrow I'll write the letter with her account number on it and send a death certificate. I'll mail everything Fed Ex Overnight.

But it's Christmas time so the insurance company won't act on my request until next week. They'll have to have that stuff in order to pay me; I'm mom's beneficiary. Whenever I get that money then I can pay off the loan on the shop. And like I remember mom telling me as she nodded, 'set enough aside for a someday education.'"

"Lindsey, you're amazing," Caleb smiled to her, "I'll be back in a couple of hours."

&

As Lindsey sat eating her favorite toasted cheese sandwich with ketchup in the middle and slurping comforting chicken noodle soup, other questions raced through her mind.

"Mom's car's totaled. I wonder if the insurance company will value the car enough so I can use the money for a used car. Yeah, she paid it off last year. I remember how proud she was to have that loan paid. Holy crud, I gotta have a car to get out to CC for my GED class. Uncle Caleb's got his own life; he can't be carting me around, especially at night."

&

Lindsey worked alone in the shop for part of the morning. Lily made deliveries. She looked up to see two young men in black uniforms walk through the shop. Outside her store she saw a parked ambulance. The men wore phones on their upper front vests. As they approached her, one of the guys turned off his phone.

Lindsey smiled. She remembered her earlier conversation about guys coming in at the last minute to get Christmas flowers for a loved one.

"Good morning, guys and Happy Holidays."

They seemed huge to her, given her small size as she looked up to them for a nametag or a name of their ambulance service.

"Happy Holidays, that's a knowing smile you have. I suspect you're aware of exactly why we are here," Brady McDern said.

Lindsey nodded, "Pretty much," she said as she gave them a lazy smile.

"So?"

"Your mom," she saw his nametag, "Brady, right?"

"You got it."

Brady smiled to her as she showed him the arrangements and prices including the delivery charge. He chose an arrangement of red and white that included one red rose and gave her the delivery address.

"This is our most popular arrangement; your mom'll love it," Lindsey said as she looked up to him. Brady turned back to his partner and gave him an eyebrow's up approval of Lindsey.

"Yup, the flower shop over in Bellton will deliver these to your mom tomorrow. Oh, I think she'll be happy. Oops, I almost forgot, would you like to send a card with it?"

Brad shook his head as he paid for the flowers.

"You from Bellton, Brady?

"Yeah, I was raised near there."

"Well, Porttown is in the middle of the state, uh, your town, about 45 miles north of here?

Brady nodded to her, "That's right," he paused, "say, does the shop have a business card I could have? Sometime I could call you up and do an order."

"Certainly, here you go, and, guys, might you have a business card for your service? I'd like to add you to our list of clients; you just never know."

Brady's partner handed the EMS card to Lindsey. Brady held The Flower Shop card.

"Your name tag says Lindsey. The card says Mariah O'Ranon?"

"That's mom; the shop's mine now."

Brady watched Lindsey nod and thought, "Wow, she looks about 14, already running a business?"

"Have a really good Christmas, guys, and thanks for stopping in."

∞

"Holy crud, Brady, he's, wow, big, powerful, nice, I love his dark brown eyes, I see light reflecting in them. I have the business card. Maybe someday I'll meet a guy like him, wow."

Lindsey shook herself out of her reverie as the phone rang. After she took the order, she logged it into the computer and went back to working on the three orders she needed to finish. Her mind stayed on Brady's order for his mom.

She rolled it over in her mind, "No card with the order, I hope he calls his mom. Gosh, maybe he can't see his mom for Christmas. He's an EMT, maybe he's on duty. Folks in the medical profession, that's a 24/7 deal. They hafta celebrate life during their precious times off duty."

∞

That evening Jen drove over to deliver her Christmas present to Lindsey.

"I hope you like what I got you, Lindsey."

"And I hope you like what I got you, Jen. Thank goodness I picked it out a while ago."

"Are you and Caleb going to church Christmas Eve?"

Lindsey shook her head, "Gosh, we haven't gotten that far. I can just barely stay ahead about 12 hours at a time."

"I would like to invite you and Caleb to midnight mass, if you'd care to come. Mom and Dad will drive us, pick you up and deliver you home. Also, we want you to come to our noon Christmas Day meal. Girl, I won't put up with you two being alone that whole day."

Lindsey broke into tears. Jen came to her, and they hugged, "Best friend, I didn't mean to make you cry."

Lindsey stepped back from her, "It's just that, it's just that, everyone is being kind to us." She shook her head, "Just didn't expect it. Thanks, Jen, I'll check with Uncle Caleb and let you know."

℘

"I'll do deliveries this Friday morning."

"Are you sure, Lindsey?"

"Yeah, I need to get out of the shop. Anybody who calls after 11:30, we won't be able to deliver flowers until Monday, the 27th. There's only so much we can do physically with last second stuff."

Lily looked over to Lindsey as she put on her outdoor shop jacket and thought, "How grownup Lindsey acts just in these past few days."

Lindsey took the time yesterday to compliment Lily on how professional she dressed at the shop. Lily wore dark slacks and a collared shirt with long sleeves in winter and short sleeves in summer. Lindsey and her mother strongly disagreed on professional dress. Mariah wore too tight blue jeans, and she let a lot of cleavage show in her choice of tops. Lindsey made up her mind to wear turtlenecks in winter and collared shirts with sleeves the rest of the time. She needed to buy several pairs of dark slacks for work. She wanted Lily's professional look for herself.

"Wow, I gotta get used to how this van drives; different from yesterday, a dusting of snow now," Lindsey spoke out as she headed for her delivery. "I know we got radials for all seasons on this guy, but I'll still slide around some."

She reviewed in her mind what her mom taught her about winter driving.

"For heaven's sake, stay back. Following too close is a recipe for disaster," Lindsey could hear her mother's voice, it seemed right next to her.

"Thanks, Mom," Lindsey chuckled.

She finished all but one of her deliveries and headed back to Porttown. The country road she drove remained snowy, not plowed. It looked as if only a few people drove it since the last snow. Ahead she saw a car in the right ditch. People lay on the ground, one in her lane and one on the shoulder. Lindsey slowed down, gently applying the brake as she eased off the pavement to an area where not much snow lay on the shoulder. She pushed the emergency lights as she stopped. When she shut off the engine, she put the van key in her pocket right away. As she approached the vehicle she noticed the open car doors.

Lindsey's track coach asked her to take CPR and First Aid. Lindsey thought that made sense so her sophomore year completed both courses.

"Sure as heck better to know this stuff instead of World History," she told coach. "I learned a lot, and, you know what, I liked it."

Coach smiled to her; he knew of her dislike for most of her classes.

Lindsey's mind tracked back through her CPR and First Aid training. Her big problem remained chest compressions. At 5'2" and 95 lbs. her compressions often weren't hard enough; it was a matter of her physical size.

She knelt next to the person with the large gash on the side of his head. Lindsey saw blood still trickling from the wound onto the snowy ground. She pulled the coat away to feel for the carotid artery in his neck. At first she felt no pulsing. Lindsey blew out a breath and inhaled. Now she felt his pulse.

"Whew, I'm so scared I couldn't feel it," she said out loud. "Can you hear me?"

"Smelled, smelled gas, so I pulled my buddy out; then I slipped and fell."

Lindsey heard a car motor behind her.

"Should I call 911?" the woman hollered out the car window.

"Yes, call," Lindsey hollered back.

Lindsey knelt next to the other person lying in the shoulder. Lindsey felt for a pulse. There was none, no breath either. She looked at the bent angle of the man's head and neck.

"Can I help?" a quiet voice asked as she knelt next to Lindsey.

"I dunno; no pulse, so I'll start chest compressions. Not gonna do anything else 'cause of suspicious head angle."

Lindsey and the woman took turns with the compressions, saying "Staying Alive" as they pressed.

Soon they heard a deep male voice from behind them, "We got it, thanks ladies."

Lindsey turned to the speaker as she got up. The emergency person nodded to her. She moved away as quick as she could as the crew lay down the equipment they needed.

"Still no pulse," she told the EMT. "The other guy's got a pulse."

Lindsey stood there thinking that she might just be looking at the first dead person she ever saw. She ran back to the person lying in the road as the second ambulance arrived.

She knelt down and felt the man's pulse.

"The bleeding's almost stopped on his head," she turned as she spoke to the EMT who knelt down next to her.

"Brady!" she said in a loud whisper. She felt her body rock at the shock of seeing him beside her.

"Lindsey, that you?"

"Yeah."

Lindsey raised up and moved away from him. She stayed on to give a report to the police, since she was the first person on the scene.

"Thank you for helping, Lindsey," Brady came up to her as he got ready to leave. He gave her a small smile and touched her shoulder.

"I'm heading out, may I call you? I'd like to share what happened here. I really want to get to know you."

Lindsey's mouth opened, but she was unable to speak. She just nodded her head to him. His ambulance took off. She watched the flashing lights but did not hear a siren. Lindsey called the shop on the van's portable phone. She explained what happened and told Lily she'd be back as soon as she dropped the flowers at the hospital. Then she would do the second and final delivery before Christmas.

"Gosh, there's lots of cars in the parking lot. I expected people would go home for the holidays. But maybe there are that many sick people here today."

Lindsey looked at herself in the rearview mirror. She brushed her hair to make herself presentable for the delivery. She stopped at the reception desk.

"We're shorthanded today, beings it's Christmas Eve," the receptionist said. "Could I ask you to please deliver the flowers for me. Otherwise they might not get to the patient until later today."

"Of course," Lindsey smiled, "just let me know the room number and I'll be happy to take these right up."

Everyone spoke in friendly tones as she made her way to the surgery wing. She stopped at the nurse's station there.

"Go ahead and take them in." The nurse read the shop name on her coat, "That's a lovely bouquet from your shop."

Lindsey smiled to the nurse. She decided there was something about fresh flowers that made people feel comfortable.

"Come in," Lindsey heard the woman's voice as she peeked around the door after she knocked.

"These are so lovely, oh here's the card. Thank you, oh flowers are wonderful for recoveries," she nodded as she smiled to Lindsey.

"Dear, these," the woman stopped, "smell divine. Thank you for bringing them up, my first flowers. Sweetie, you'll have a Merry Christmas, OK?"

All Lindsey could do was give the woman a small smile. She walked out of the room with tears in her eyes.

"What a nice woman, thinking of me while she lies in that hospital bed, wishing me a Merry Christmas," Lindsey spoke out in a soft voice.

As Lindsey left the floor and headed for the elevator she took a good look around.

"This hospital is a pleasant place; lots of people get well. There're positive vibes I'm picking up here," she thought.

Lindsey gave the same hard look around as she walked through the main reception area. Folks were being tended to in the admitting cubicles she just passed.

"I wonder, I just wonder, would I like helping folks get well?" she whispered.

As she walked out of the main hospital entrance she looked to the right and saw two ambulances backed up, one at the emergency room delivery door, and the second one next to it.

"Green," she thought, "I don't remember the name, but Brady's ambulance had a lot of green on it. Wow, he may be right in there, taking care of his patient, turning him over to the ER staff. No doubt, those guys help save a bunch of lives. But some do die."

Lindsey kept walking toward the shop van, parked in a designated delivery area. She stopped, "Mom, you didn't make it."

Tears flooded her face as she tried to insert the key into the van door. She gave up trying and leaned into the van and cried. After several minutes she started to recover.

∞

Lily and Caleb helped her put two more flower arrangements in the van for the afternoon delivery. The three of them decided yesterday to close the shop at 3:30. Family Christmas services would start soon on this Christmas Eve. When Lindsey returned she gave Lily her Christmas present from Mariah.

"Thanks Lindsey," Lily said, "your mom always thought about others, before herself. You and Caleb done great here; it will quiet down next week. We do have all the flowers to arrange for Country Club events, and there's a wedding. That's what's comin' up plus the new flooring."

"I'm happy to be busy, and next week I promised I'd do the painting," Lindsey said as she hugged Lily.

"Caleb, head out as soon as you sweep up. I'll walk; I need to clear my head."

Earlier Lindsey took a shop money deposit to the bank.

"We'll be clear of cash; I intend to do that every day from now on, deposit daily; mom thought three times a week was enough. It's just five doors down to the bank," she told Caleb and Lily after she made that decision.

Lindsey looked up at the darkening sky as she walked home. Huge stars popped up into the heavens, more as she moved along. Then she remembered. "My birthday's gone, my 16th; no card, no cake, nothing. But the most important thing happened; I got my driver's license."

℘

Lindsey felt an achy jab in her heart as she unlocked her front door. Her home smelled fresher as she took in a deep breath. She decided that cleaning up was worth it. She smelled coffee brewed in the kitchen. She found her uncle doing laundry.

"Hey, Uncle Caleb, what do you want to do about tonight?"

"Hope it's all right, I called Jen and told her we'd be happy to join her family for midnight mass. I've attended a couple of those masses, pretty neat. Anyway I love Christmas."

"Thanks, I just couldn't decide about what to do."

Lindsey put her stuff in her room and headed for the kitchen. She washed her hands and poured herself a partial cup of coffee.

Caleb joined her and poured himself a cup.

"Jen asked me about Christmas dinner at noon tomorrow. I said yes, OK?"

"That's fine, thanks Uncle Caleb, for pushing me along. What I really want to do is go to bed and never get up again. But that's not good, being depressed, I think that would be my anger turned inward, we just gotta go on, a lot of life to live, right?"

"You got it, honey bear."

ᔆᕽ

"What a beautiful service, thanks Mr. and Mrs. Dempsey, for bringing us along for midnight mass."

"My favorite part," Caleb admitted as the family neared the O'Ranon home, "was the singing while we held our lit candles."

"Ours too," the whole family spoke in unison.

Jen asked, "We'd like you to come over about 11:30. The meal will be at noon. No, we don't want you to bring anything, just yourselves, OK?"

"You're sure?" Lindsey questioned Jen.

"We're positive," Mrs. Dempsey assured them. "We want you to relax, something you don't have any idea about, for a while now, running the business."

ᔆᕽ

"Two whole days off, unbelievable," Lindsey spoke out as she showered. After she dressed she made coffee and fixed a cup of hot chocolate for herself.

She and her uncle agreed to sleep in and just have donuts as they opened their presents. They knew a sumptuous meal awaited them at noon. Caleb started a fire; Lindsey took presents from under the tree and handed Caleb his. Earlier she pulled a recliner close to the fire for him.

"I didn't know what to do with Mariah's presents. Want to open them?"

"Yeah, mom's with us in spirit, sittin' right beside us, so we need to show her what she got."

"Right."

After Lindsey opened her and Mariah's presents, she had to laugh.

Both Lindsey and Lily purchased turtlenecks for Mariah. And they didn't check in with each other about that. They just both wanted Mariah to have a more professional look at work.

"Uncle Caleb, both Lily and me wanted mom to dress up a little more."

"Hey, can't you wear the turtlenecks?"

"Uh huh, they'll be a little large, but I gotta have them for wearin' at the shop. I just don't have enough stuff."

ॐ

Jen's parents got Lindsey and Caleb to laugh. They relaxed and enjoyed the wonderful meal: ham, scalloped potatoes, green bean casserole, veggie tray, and rolls.

"We saw you in your military uniform at the funeral. Want to share about your experience in the Army?"

Caleb gazed around at the family and then at Lindsey.

"Uh, not used to talking about my experience. But you're like family," he smiled to everyone, "so I guess."

Caleb went on to tell of his six years in the Army and his six months spent in Afghanistan.

"I really believe I left Afghanistan a better place than I found it. We put up that school in the village, wow, in such a short time. I've never seen such excited little kids, getting to go back to school."

He shared about his accident and the six month recuperation at Walter Reed.

"I want you to see my great lower leg."

He stood up from the table and pulled up the leg of his tan pants.

"They did a terrific job with me, the prosthetics folks and the physical therapists. The emotional trauma of the accident, well, I'll always have to work on that, but I had real good care from the mental health folks at the hospital.

Mariah came to see me twice. She suggested that I come live with her and Lindsey when I finally got released, first from the hospital and then from the Army."

Jen's family thanked him for his military service after he sat down. Jen's dad mentioned the strong VFW unit in the Porttown community.

"I've already gotten to know some of the men in that Post; they really understand what happens to us in war. All I know is that this one, this conflict, it'll go on for a long time," he nodded to them. "I'll try to help out; I know that wounded warriors are starting to band together across the country. That's what we're called, wounded warriors."

℘

Jen left the dinner table and returned several minutes later holding a cake with 16 lighted candles.

Lindsey heard the singing of *Happy Birthday*. After she made her wish and blew out the candles, she burst into tears. She could not control her crying and finally excused herself from the table for a little while. She returned, apologizing for her tears.

"Thank you, oh thank you."

Jen handed her a plate with cake on it.

"Carrot, my favorite, oh wow. Sometimes, stuff touches my heart, like you folks and your consideration for me, for my special day, on top of Christmas, thank you for your kindness," she tried to smile as her eyes went from person to person.

"And Jen, heartfelt thanks to you for my necklace."

Lindsey picked up the necklace she wore and showed everyone the small heart attached to the necklace. She looked at Jen and patted her hand over her heart.

"Reminds me of you, Jen," Lindsey paused and swallowed, "and of mom."

Jen nodded back to Lindsey.

&

"Mom, you are my model of a business person. And you are my hero. You knew what you wanted and you went for it. You did it anyway, you lived, and loved, and I know you prayed, a lot. I also feel you want me to do the right thing with your stuff. So, I'm giving it all to groups that help the less fortunate."

Lindsey pulled her mom's bedroom curtains open after she spoke out. The sun shone, making the white snow even more gleaming as she looked outside. Lindsey remembered thinking about the lack of sun a week ago as she left church. This Sunday she wanted to stay home, to take care of several projects related to her mom.

"We go on, mom," Lindsey blew out a breath as she began her task in the now sunshiny bedroom.

Lindsey made piles, clean clothes and coats for donation, clothes that needed washing for donating, shoes and handbags and miscellaneous clothing from drawers and the closet shelves to decide on.

Caleb took inventory as he sat in a chair in Mariah's bedroom. Lindsey loaded the washer with dirty clothes. They tag teamed and finished the effort in 45 minutes. While Mariah's clothes dried, they attacked the garage, deciding what to trash and what could be given away. Caleb kept up his inventory effort.

"Uncle Caleb, one more place, the study, when you have time, please go through everything. I'll let you decide what's important; gotta keep mom's personal tax folders from the past few years. Most everythin' else is in her notebook. I'll keep that in her closet, where she kept it."

"Pizza?"

"Yeah, I'm exhausted, Uncle Caleb, we done a lot today. Hey, I bought several pizzas. Which kind do you want me to bake?"

"Up to you."

∞

That night they watched a Christmas movie as they ate their pizza.

"Lindsey, tomorrow I'm not going in to the shop, OK?"

"What's up?"

"I gotta see my counselor and go back to PT; I stopped that to help you. Anyhow, tomorrow the landlord is putting in new linoleum all over the shop, right?"

"Right, it's a job for Monday and Tuesday, and I'm painting a couple of walls. I told mom I would help out. The landlord's taking a little off our January rent 'cause I'm doing painting for him. He brought the paint, roller, pan and brushes over a couple weeks ago. He called and asked if I wanted to postpone the project after mom died. I told him it would help us all to brighten up the shop, make it like new. That stuff has to be done this week after Christmas 'cause I start the GED right after New Year's." Lindsey paused, "You know we got a huge holiday comin' up, almost bigger than Christmas."

"Uh huh, Valentine's Day, Mariah told me about the small semi they unhook out in the back alley; unbelievable how many roses that thing must hold."

"Yeah, and we sell them all; roses come in, no kidding, from Miami and before that from countries like Columbia and Ecuador, all to help us with our romantic fixation with roses, and romance and Valentine's Day."

3

By 10:30 that Monday morning the new linoleum lay over the ugly old flooring in the front half of the shop. Lindsey painted the wall along the left side of the shop. She liked the color the landlord picked out with Mariah, a pale green, calming. The landlord supervised the moving around of all the shop's equipment, keeping ahead of the flooring people.

"Phone, it's for you, Lindsey," Lily hollered out from the back.

She had about ten minutes of painting left to do in the front area. Then she would move to the back walls that needed painting.

"The Flower Shop, this is Lindsey, how may I help you?"

"Hi Lindsey, this is Brady McDern, I'm the EMT at the accident you helped with on Christmas Eve."

Lindsey began to tremble, her mind racing back to that terrible scene.

"Hi, hi, uh Brady," her voice shook as she spoke into the phone.

"Remember I told you I would get back to you about the folks you helped. I'm going to be in Porttown on Wednesday. I would like you to come to lunch with me. I have an hour and a half free. Then I'm back on duty."

"Uh, sure, Brady, thanks, I accept. Uh, tell me quick, did the one man survive?"

"No, Lindsey, he didn't."

A sob escaped Lindsey's throat and her voice wavered, "Please tell me what time to meet?"

"I'll pick you up at 11."

"I'll have the shop covered so I can step away for a bit. Thanks, Brady."

"Lookin' forward to seeing you, Lindsey," he spoke to her in the same comforting way she heard at the accident scene.

℘

"Unbelievable, Lindsey, wow, everything looks so clean, the earth colors in the flooring and the pale green walls, I like it, like stepping into a patio area, complete with the plant smells," Caleb smiled to her as he looked around on Tuesday afternoon.

"I'm glad you took time away, Uncle Caleb. And I'm glad you like it. Chet, our landlord, sure was impressed with how much better plants and flowers present when floors and walls look fresh."

Lily spent Tuesday afternoon going through the decorations for the various holidays that were used in the front windows.

"Some of this stuff is really old, from the previous shop owners. Do you want me to decide what to keep and what to toss?"

"Yup, Lily, you know best; I'm just learning how to decorate the front windows, what looks good. Tomorrow we start on the wedding flowers, and all the stuff to get the country club ready for New Year's Eve festivities."

Caleb and Lily would cover for Lindsey on Wednesday so she could have lunch away from the shop.

∽

"Why am I so scared?" Lindsey kept asking herself as she worked through the flower arrangement in front of her. "Maybe it's because I'm standin' on my own two feet, as an adult, not some high school kid. Brady, I liked him instantly. Maybe it's what he does, I dunno."

She shook her head. Today she wore a deep red turtleneck with black slacks. Getting ready that morning she decided on a bit of mascara and light pink lipstick.

At 11:00 Brady strode into the shop. He looked around a bit and gazed to the back. Lindsey stood there, smiling at him. She introduced him to her uncle and then to Lily.

"Have a good lunch," Caleb said as they headed out of the shop.

Lindsey waved back.

As they walked down the freshly shoveled sidewalk, he asked, "How are you, Lindsey?"

"So much to tell you, Brady, and how are you?"

"Same, so much to say, an hour and a half's not long enough."

She turned her head to look up at him and watched his eyes smile.

"Here we are, food's good, not too crowded yet."

They picked a back booth that was more private. They agreed to order first, so they could eat and talk, and then talk.

Lindsey spoke out, "I gotta know," she paused and Brady saw her clench her hands together, "I prayed so hard, when I first looked at the man we did CPR on, uh, his head and neck, looked like his neck, broken?"

"That's right, the coroner figures that the man pulling the other man from the car, somehow that action broke the one man's neck, or finished breaking his neck."

"Then he's in God's hands," Lindsey looked across the table, her eyes penetrating Brady's. She nodded as tears came to her eyes.

Brady asked her to share first. Lindsey spoke in rapid phrases, wanting to get everything she wanted to say out, so Brady would know her situation, including her accident encounter. She told him about her track coach urging her to take CPR and First Aid.

"He musta saw somethin' in me, somethin' I can't see in myself. All I know is I always helped when there was a track teammate who got injured. I am so glad I got the training."

Brady watched a small smile light her face.

"So you just turned 16. And you run a business, a very labor intensive one, to keep your mom's dream alive. And you'll finish your education and decide then what you want. And you asked my advice about a way to get to your classes."

"Yeah, but, before advice, I want to hear about you. And," she let out a deep breath, "I want to tell you how much I appreciate what you EMT's do, saving lives. You're angels, straight from God," she nodded as she smiled to him.

He watched tears form in her green eyes and thought, "She's for real, cares, understands."

His brown eyes penetrated her green ones as he spoke.

"I love what I do; I've always wanted to be in rescue, in some way. I'm 22, took my EMT training right out of high school. But I wanted more."

Their food arrived. They ate and Brady ate and talked between bites.

"I'm at the U of I, in Iowa City, last phase of paramedic training, in the middle of my field internship of 450 hours. I began in August with the medical training and I'll finish," he stopped and looked up, "God willing, in June when I take both the National and Iowa Registries for Paramedics. Passing that, I'm a paramedic."

"You bring people back from the dead, out on our highways and byways,"

"Not all," he shook his head, "not all, Lindsey."

Her voice cracked as she replied, "Yeah, I sure know that."

"Right now, I'm on reserve for two weeks. I do reserve work plus my field internship."

Lindsey shook her head, not understanding.

"Last week, Christmas week and this week, I'm filling in as an EMT reserve in this district so a married EMT can spend time with his family. This EMT district is not too far from where I grew up."

"Bellton, right?"

Brady smiled to her, "Bellton, you remembered."

Lindsey nodded, "Yeah, I called the florist in Bellton after you left, remember you giving me your mom's address." Lindsey smiled, "And did your mom like what you ordered for her?"

"Wow, yeah, really she did. Hey, the picture didn't do the arrangement justice; it's much prettier. I celebrated Christmas with her one evening after Christmas, when I got a little time off. The arrangement, really touched her, she had tears, thanking me."

"Yeah, moms love flowers."

"Lindsey, I am so sorry, for you and your uncle's loss."

She looked into his eyes, "Thanks, Brady." She collected her thoughts and said, "So you know my crazy high school story, tell me about your earlier days."

"Farm kid, disliked the life style, my twin brother, Jared, loved the ag stuff. I wanted no part of it when I graduated high school. Jared runs the corn operation now. Dad died when we were 20. Mom moved to town. She's like me," Lindsey watched him make an ugly face, "wanted another life. We're happy now," he paused and nodded, "my family is. But it was a rough patch, especially for me, family wanted me to be a vet. I wanted to work with people in medical distress, not animals. And I didn't thrive on the classroom paramedic medical training like I'm doing out in the field internship. I love the being outside the four walls of a hospital setting, applying what I've learned. The sun, the roads, the heat, the cold, that's my groove, totally."

"How in the world do you calm down that adrenaline flow after you leave the emergency room?"

"Good question," Lindsey watched him nod and smile to her, "music, all kinds, calms me; I sleep like a rock, like I'm plain knocked out. I wake up the same way, in fourth gear, ready to rock and roll."

"I'm gonna need a car, what's your advice, Brady?"

"The car insurance company, it'll take time to get their check so you can buy a car. Your mom's estate, it's in probate?"

"Yeah, but our lawyer said it would be pretty quick."

"If I were you, I'd start looking for what you might want, given the money you want to spend. Yeah, have a car in mind, so when the moula arrives, you'll be ready to act."

"Gosh, I hadn't even thought about that; I'm so obsessed about the money, same deal with the life insurance money, payin' stuff off."

"You'll have to ask your uncle for his assistance in driving you or ask him to borrow his car; how many nights a week is your GED class?"

"Monday through Thursday, do you think I've taken on too much, Brady?"

He shook his head, "You're smart, those are super PSAT scores you shared with me, and National Merit Scholarship contention, that's something, Lindsey."

"I lack confidence right now."

Brady smiled, "Hey, I think you're pretty confident, the way you sailed through your chat with me that convinced me of what I needed to get mom. You already got PR and salesmanship down solid."

There was a short pause, as each of them tried to take in all that they heard from each other.

"Right now, I try to plan ahead, where I want to be as a paramedic, what I want for my personal life. I been in school for," he nodded his head, "like forever. It's been two years since the one relationship I've had with a woman. When she finally realized the life style an EMT has, she said so long. You?"

He stopped and shook his head, "Hey, it's none of my business."

"My first love, fell hard, one sexual encounter with him," she shook her head, "he walked away, said no way, no commitment for him."

"I'm sorry, Lindsey."

"For the best," she looked, searching his eyes, "God's got a special plan for me. I felt pieces of that plan, when mom died."

"He has that for all of us, Lindsey, I believe that."

"I believe that too."

ℰↄ

They held hands as they returned to The Flower Shop. Lindsey showed him her world, the new flooring, painted walls, all the flowers being arranged for the wedding and the New Year's Eve celebration coming up.

"I try to be an artisan, Brady, creating beauty with living things. Lily has great training in flowers so I rely on her judgment on so much of what we do, especially pricing. She's the real artisan."

Lindsey went to Lily who stood by the cash register. She gave Lily a hug and a "Thanks for all you do."

"I have just a couple minutes; you asked if you could look into the back of the ambulance. I saw walking back that my partner parked the ambulance a couple of cars down."

Lindsey peeked into the back of the ambulance, loaded with foreign looking lifesaving pieces of equipment. She asked if she could sit in the passenger seat in the front. Everything around her seemed large. Then she remembered her small size.

"Thanks for lunch, Brady, I hope we can see each other again. I've got your advice tucked into my brain."

"We will see each other again, Lindsey," Brady's eyes beamed down into hers.

"Hug?"

"Yes," as he enclosed his big frame around her. She felt his warmth as he kissed her on the top of her head.

"Be safe."

"You too, Lindsey."

She backed away and stepped up on the curb. She stopped and waved to him.

ℰↄ

Two days after Lindsey began her GED prep work she received a call from a counselor at the community college.

"Lindsey, hi, I'm Ava Penton. I work with the faculty who teach the GED prep course at Porttown CC. Your teacher showed me your card of information you filled out the first night of class. You have outstanding PSAT scores. On the card you indicated that you also want to prep for the SAT and the ACT. The card says you disliked high school, boredom is what you put down for a reason."

"That's right, I didn't put this down on the card, but I'm running my mom's florist business. That's why my work number is on the card plus our home number. I'm not home much. My mom, she died before Christmas, car accident. So far I'm liking the GED work; no messin' around, which is what I want. Seems like I wasted so much time sitting in those high school classrooms. I don't feel that way at all, in the GED classroom now; I'll push myself as hard as I can. I want that GED. And I want those ACT and SAT scores, good ones for if and when I decide to go on to school."

"I compliment you on the goals you've set for yourself. And I am so sorry to hear about your mom. So you work full time at your florist shop?"

"Right, Mrs. Penton, is it?"

"It is, Mrs."

"Yes, full time, Monday through Friday, 9 to 5 and Saturday until 3:30 p.m. I found a little time yesterday to study while I ate my lunch. It's amazing how much time I used to waste."

"Lindsey, how old are you?"

"I turned 16, right before Christmas."

"We'll chat again. Your teacher has high hopes for you."

℘

Jen stopped by the shop one Saturday morning in late January. Lindsey greeted her with a hug and a humongous smile on her face.

"You look happy, really happy. We haven't talked like forever."

"I know, Jen, I love GED prep. I'm burnin' through the work, my teacher's letting me fly. Oh Jen, I really like my teacher."

Jen watched tears form in Lindsey's eyes, "She, she shines a light of hope, of possibility into this dark time of my life."

Lindsey stopped for a minute and cried.

She wiped her eyes with her tissue and began to smile, "Ms. Townsend, she says I could be ready to take the test by early April, can you believe it, I'll be done, at 16."

"You're studying for the ACT and SAT, too, right?"

"Uh huh, I try to divide my time up, 20% exam board prep time, 80% GED prep time. Jen, each day is so precious, and we don't," Lindsey dropped her head, then raised up, "we don't get time back. It's gone; what we're doin' right now, that's gotta count, in a big way."

Jen gave Lindsey a thoughtful look, her eyes concentrating on Lindsey's, "You've really grown up, a maturity I haven't seen before. This is the Lindsey, hey, that I thought you could be."

Jen hugged her friend again.

"I gotta go."

"I've met someone, Jen, I'll share more later, school's good?"

Jen nodded.

"You'll help us with Valentine's Day again this year?"

"I sure will; it was a rockin' good time last year; are you guys getting the refrigerated semi for the roses?"

Lindsey smiled to her friend, "Sheez, you remembered, yeah, we are. And of course I'll pay you. Mom wrote out such specific instructions for the day. It's a Monday this year. That's so awesome 'cause we can get so much done the day before."

"And get everything delivered on Monday," Jen added.

"Where we can I want to make Sunday deliveries."

Jen turned and waved as she left the shop. Lindsey waved back.

ಐ

Caleb helped her pick it out, a light gray Honda two door, six years old. He took her to three different dealerships the two late Thursday afternoons before. Lindsey wanted reliability. The car had low mileage. And she paid for it with life insurance money. The car insurance company finally decided on the depreciated value of Mariah's totaled vehicle.

"Uncle Caleb, I can't believe how much it costs to have wheels. I gotta pay for my plates and vehicle registration plus car insurance. I appreciate you signing as my guardian so I could get the car insurance."

Caleb smiled to her, "Uh, that's what guardians do."

"Yeah, and I'm sure glad mom's insurance company came through with the funds they owed me as beneficiary. Otherwise, I wouldn't have enough to swing this car deal. It'll be a while before I get a check from mom's car insurance company."

"Living is pretty expensive, Lindsey."

"Yeah, as I saw the life insurance money fly out of my account to the bank to pay off the loan. Now we got the shop and the shop van free and clear. And thanks to your budgeting plus the help of Jen's dad, I have money set aside to go on to school someday. Mom never talked about it, what you said, how expensive everything was, just living. How did she do it?"

"Honey bear, a lot of sacrifice, you never saw it, but she did without a lot in order to make your life a good one. It's time I told you. Your mom socked every penny from her part of the divorce settlement with your dad into this business."

"I don't understand, Uncle Caleb."

Caleb noticed the solemn look on his niece's face.

"When your home sold, your mom got half the net proceeds on the home your family had and your dad got the other half. Mariah put a large portion as a down payment to buy this business, the flower shop. You moved to a place, less expensive, the small rental. You needed a home, Lindsey. Your mom gave you a good one."

"Gosh, she never explained all that to me with that kind of detail."

"You were a kid with a dad who walked out of your life, and a mom who had a dream for your futures. She wanted you to have friends, to be happy. It didn't take long though, after she got into the business, well she needed more help. At 13 you became that help. Lily was important too."

"Hey I wanted to be here. I loved it here at the shop and disliked school. Working here just made good sense to me, helpin' out."

"How do you feel about GED prep?"

"I love it, I eat it up, don't have to wait for anybody, work at my own pace, my teacher checks on me. Wow, she is so encouraging, doesn't look at me like my teachers did, with disdain. They knew I was smart, but my teachers couldn't motivate me. Regular school, that just wasn't me," Lindsey shook her head and let out a big sigh.

§⊃

Lindsey decided to drive to church that Sunday morning after she made coffee and had a chocolate donut, her special treat on Sundays. Caleb slept late.

"I won't wake him; he's been restless at night lately," she said out loud as she backed her car out of the garage, got out and looked around at the items that remained in the garage. Caleb's pickup, a lawn mower, a few tools and miscellaneous stuff stayed; the rest Lindsey gave to the nonprofits for the needy.

She nodded as in her mind she whizzed through all the items given to someone else.

"Caleb, I couldn't have done all this without your help; you're awesome. When I get back from church, I need to tell you that," she spoke out.

She pulled the garage door down and headed for church. Reverend Tompkin delivered a spot-on message regarding risk and love. He spoke about loving God and loving your neighbor as you love yourself.

It really hit her when he said it, "It's a brave heart that risks being broken to discover the joy of love."

"That's me," she told herself as she drove home, "I will take risks, I want love in my life, want to know Brady."

Brady took another EMS reserve job, this time just a long weekend. He and Lindsey planned to spend a Sunday afternoon together, before the Monday of President's Day. Lindsey left her car out in the driveway after she got home from church. She walked up to the front door of her home. The wreath still looked nice; she touched the needles. She felt brittleness setting in.

"Strange," she thought as she smelled the coffee she brewed before she left. She checked the pot. Caleb hadn't had a cup. Lindsey walked back past Mariah's bedroom and put her coat on her bed. She decided to knock on her uncle's door. It was not like him to sleep in that late.

There was no response.

"Hey Uncle Caleb, sleepy head, get up, get up, daylight's burnin'."

It was a favorite phrase her uncle said to her when she slept in.

A white flash crossed her eyes; she remembered seeing the car in the ditch. What she felt then, a terrible heat, she felt now. She turned the handle on the door. It opened easily, not locked. Caleb's curtains remained closed. She turned on the light and did not see him lying in bed.

"Uncle Caleb?"

She took two steps forward and saw him lying on the floor, on the other side of the bed. She squeezed into the space between the bed and the wall. She felt like she was burning up, even her fingers burned. Lindsey leaned up and touched his neck. Again, her burning finger did not find a pulse. She slid her hand down on his chest and waited for him to inhale and exhale.

Nothing.

Lindsey called 911 and returned to his room. In slow motion because of the weight she moved the bed over so she could get close enough to him to start CPR. She undid his shirt and started the compressions. Tears poured from her eyes; her hands felt firm as she kept up the chest compressions. After a time she heard the wail of emergency vehicles. She felt the sticky sweat starting to run down her face.

"I locked the front door, sorry Uncle Caleb, I got to go unlock it, don't want them bustin' down the door."

She returned and continued the compressions.

"Where are you folks?" an emergency person spoke out as he walked into the house.

"Back bedroom," Lindsey hollered out.

"Let us take over, OK?"

The paramedic spoke in a quiet voice to her as he stood over her and her uncle.

Tears flowed so hard down Lindsey's face that she had trouble catching her breath. A fireman held her hand as he helped her get up. He guided her as they walked out of Caleb's room, down the hall and into the kitchen.

"Coffee?"

She nodded her head as he handed her paper towels to mop her face and nose. After she drank part of the cup, he asked what happened. She told him what little she knew, that she let Caleb sleep in while she went to church.

"Sir, I couldn't feel his pulse, or a breath. I know CPR. He's my uncle, back from the war, injured. We've been so proud of how he's done since he moved in with mom and me."

"Your mom, will she be home soon?"

The fireman watched fresh tears wash down Lindsey's face.

Lindsey looked across to him, her voice small and quiet, "Mom is home," she paused, "with God, in heaven."

Lindsey's eyes cleared as she watched the color drain from the fireman's face.

"I'm so sorry."

"Mom died the week before Christmas, a head on."

The paramedics revived Caleb. Lindsey watched them take him to the ambulance on their gurney.

"Can we call someone for you, Lindsey?"

She looked at the fireman who continued to stay by her side, "Thanks, it's OK, I'll call my friend, Jen. If I can reach her, I know she'll meet me at the hospital. Thanks for your help sir, uh, what's your name?"

"Joe, from the fire district here in Porttown."

"You're the only Joe?"

He nodded his head.

"The police are almost finished. They'll talk to you also."

Within two hours Lindsey stood on one side of her uncle's bed, and Jen stood on the other side. His hospital room remained quiet, save the beep of the heart monitor.

Caleb shook his head as tears came to his eyes.

"I thought I would end it all. God decided different. I'm glad I'm still alive."

Lindsey sobbed as she kissed him on the forehead, "We'll let you sleep."

"What now?" Lindsey asked Jen as they sat in the medical wing reception area.

"Work for you tomorrow, Lindsey; school for me; we're not spoiled little kids anymore, gotta step up."

"Right, sheez, it's gonna be tough, Lily planned on taking time off after Valentine's Day. I hope Uncle Caleb'll be well enough to help out."

"Hey, what if he's not."

"It'll be me, then. I can do this, Jen. And go to night class, and study. I been awful spoiled, like you said, and not very grateful for everything I've had. I gotta think about how lucky I've been, having a friend like you, having decent brains which I gotta start using to the max."

Lindsey watched Jen look her over, her eyes serious and her mouth in a grim line, "Yes, use your brains."

Lindsey put her head in her hands and burst into tears, "Jen, I'm scared," she said as she looked over to her friend, "And what about Uncle Caleb?"

"I'm going to be a medical doctor someday, so I'll say the medical staff will do everything they can for Caleb, that's what I'd tell my patient's family. What I won't be able to tell them I can still say to you, Lindsey, Caleb is in God's hands; God will decide. We just do what we can to help."

"I'll pray like crazy for him."

They stood up together and hugged.

"Lindsey, that's the best thing you can do. Call me, I can help."

"Yeah, Valentine's Day is just two weeks from tomorrow."

Jen stepped back from Lindsey, "That's my best bud, see, you're thinkin' ahead to that huge holiday for your business."

℘

"Thank you Lindsey for bringing me home from the hospital. What I did was just plum stupid, swallowing all that pain medication I didn't use after they released me from Walter Reed. I told you I was glad to be alive, when you and Jen were by my bed. And I am glad; I'll not pull that stunt again. I'm stepping up my counseling sessions with the psychologist. And we'll visit with Reverend Tompkin again. Then I'll go alone."

Lindsey glanced over to him as she drove.

"I love you, Caleb. We got each other."

Caleb touched her shoulder, "And I love you, I won't let you down, I gotta figure where I'm headed."

Caleb watched her nod as she said, "And I gotta figure out what's ahead for me."

ॐ

"Thank goodness we were able to come in on Sunday and get prepared,"

Lindsey smiled to Lily on the Tuesday after Valentine's Day.

"It was wild and crazy and I loved it. We all pitched in, and I had fun, Lindsey. We did it, Caleb, you, me, Jen, my buddies, Jeff and Pete, and it was a bigger sales revenue day than we had last year. Your mom'd be so proud," Lily smiled to her.

"Hey, mom was with us every step of the way. Her excellent instructions she left us saved our butts. Sometimes on Valentine's Day, even on deliveries, I could feel her right next to me. You know what?"

"Nah, what?" Lily asked.

"I felt her smiling."

Lily came around the counter and hugged Lindsey.

"Wow!"

ॐ

When Brady called and asked Lindsey what she wanted to do for their date Sunday afternoon, she suggested roller skating.

"Great," Brady replied, "that'll be some good exercise; it's been awhile since I've done that. I ice skate; there's a lake on my family's property that we used to skate on."

Excitement filled Lindsey's head as she put her gear by the front door. When Brady arrived, they hugged.

"It's so good to see you, Brady," Lindsey spoke as they stepped back from their hug.

"Been way to long, Lindsey, I missed you," he said as his brown eyes sparked into hers.

Lindsey felt a little jolt fly through her body as he spoke.

"Uncle Caleb, we're ready to head out. See you in a few hours."

She heard her uncle holler out from his bedroom, "Have a great time."

Brady looked around Lindsey's home as they got ready to leave. He got so used to making an instant assessment of a home: dark areas, furniture in the way, clutter, filth, haphazard small rugs, too many extension cords in use, so many dangers in the homes of the people he helped. He saw none of that in this tiny, neat and clean home.

"Who keeps your home up, Lindsey?"

"I do, Uncle Caleb's a neat nick too."

"On top of everything else?"

"Yeah, I'm organized and efficient, that's what it takes, same thing with the shop, it's just organization and follow through, always follow through."

As he opened the door of his small SUV to help Lindsey in, he asked, "When did you get so much common sense, kinda knowin' how to survive well?"

"After mom decided she needed me in the shop, I been workin' with adults for a while now. I know how they think."

She turned to Brady as they drove off, "I just didn't agree with adults all the time."

"Your teachers?"

"Yeah, but now, my CC instructor, wow, she's awesome."

"You've found your place, somethin' in your comfort zone."

"Wow, Brady, you understand, guess when you see people at the edge of their lives," she stopped talking, unable to continue.

"Yeah, the sick folks in my ambulance, they teach me to do the best I can with what I'm dealing with, their lives."

They roller skated around and around the rink, most of the time holding hands. After a half hour they took a break and drank pop, sitting across from each other at a small table in the bright noisy facility.

"Brady, you have a huge responsibility to your patients. I'm just gonna stick my nose where it don't belong, and you don't have to answer. Sheez, I pay out a gob for insurance, health for me, on my wheels, on our shop contents, uh, liability insurance on the shop, and insurance on the little bit of property in our rental home."

She stopped talking and looked into Brady's eyes.

She watched him nod to her, his eyes sparkling brown, "Yeah, reading your mind," he paused, "uh huh, I'll have to have malpractice insurance as soon as I'm certified. Right now, I'm covered under the umbrella of my paramedic program."

"Ooohhh, that'll be expensive, right?"

"Uh huh, but I'll have a decent salary."

"Where do you want to practice as a paramedic?"

"I'd like to stay in the eastern part of the state of Iowa, the medical setting at U of I, that's the area, within 60-80 miles of Iowa City. But I gotta be able to find that job I want."

"Brady," she looked with intent into his eyes.

"What's that, Lindsey?"

"I have a couple of nice neighbors. I think one is interested in my uncle. But this other neighbor, she's a nurse at Porttown's hospital. She and I talked. I kinda told her of my immediate plans. She's suggested I might want to think about nursing as a profession. Medical just never crossed my mind. But I'm starting to," she nodded as she smiled to him, "think about it, I gotta do work that helps people."

"Good for you, Lindsey, what about the shop?"

"Yeah, that place is really 24/7, like a hospital, can't ever escape all that goes into running a small business, the IRS, our CPA. And Lily talked to me about someone who is interested in the shop, maybe of buying me out. How do you think mom would feel about doing that with her dream?"

Brady took her small hand and placed his large hand over hers.

"Dear one, may I call you that?"

She nodded to him.

"You got a lot of guilt, trying to do what was your mom's dream. But this is your life Lindsey, yours to live as you see fit."

Brady watched the tears shimmering in Lindsey's eyes. She swallowed hard and furrowed her forehead.

"Yeah, I haf to have time, work my plan, uh, that's me and God's plan.

I'm thinkin' now my goal is to work the shop until the end of this year, 2005, then I dunno, if it'll sell, go on to school. I'm excited about my future."

"Skate again?"

They stood up and roller skated another half hour. Brady took her to a restaurant on the way back to her home.

"Your turn to talk, Brady," Lindsey said as they sat across from each other in a booth.

"Knockin' out my hours to finish my field training internship, I continue to review all my coursework from my medical training, the first part of my paramedic training. I'm done with my clinicals, that's what I did before the field training. That was tough, applying everything I learned in medical, clinicals were all at one hospital. I had patients, from the time they arrived until they left the hospital. I was doing pretty much what the interns from the medical school were doing. It was huge," he paused as he nodded to Lindsey, "I felt just like them, a practicing almost doctor."

They ordered a brownie with vanilla ice cream on top and chocolate syrup with whipping cream on top of the ice cream creation with two spoons and two coffees.

"Brady, I've seen the shows on the tube, and watching the paramedics at the accident site, you guys are flat out doctors."

Brady nodded, "Yeah, it's life or death, sometimes."

"You hafta play God."

Lindsey watched as Brady's eyes turned almost black, his jawline set in a stern look. All he could do was nod.

"This is all pretty heavy stuff, Lindsey. I hope you will start having some fun in your life."

"Not so much now, but I used to run like the wind. I'm tryin' to get back into that, but it's hard since I'm on my feet all the time at the shop. I love music, listen to all kinds, have an especial place in my heart," she stopped, "for a country star from the past, George Strait. He's my idea of a fine man, and he can sing. He sings a song about a little boy who calls himself the luckiest boy alive, that this is the best day of his life."

Lindsey stopped for a minute and nodded her head, "So many songs have great words. Oh, and I have a special girlfriend, Jen, who's been with me every step of the way through our teenage years so far. She's going to be a medical doctor, known that since she was ten."

"You're lucky to have a friend like that," he smiled to her.

They finished up the brownie and concluded the dessert was wonderful, as both of them liked chocolate.

"I really really like you, Lindsey. You've got a maturity I don't see in many grown women, especially in the university setting where I've been the last few months. You've been through so much."

"And I like you," she paused as she looked into his eyes, "a lot, Brady. I want to see you again. I realize you won't have reserve duty for a while. And my hope is that you accomplish the hours to finish up your field training, and take the tests for the paramedic registries." Lindsey stopped, "Then there's our ages, six years younger than you, haven't even graduated from high school yet."

"You mean, haven't gotten your GED yet."

"Right, Brady, that's right. But you know what?"

"Tell me."

"I'll likely take my GED by the middle of April and my SAT and ACT right after that. Gosh, that'll be the same time as the kids in my junior class take the tests. But I'll be done."

"I sense pride as I hear you say that, Lindsey."

"I, yeah, I am proud of all that I'm doing. I never dreamed," she paused again and shook her head, "oh nothing."

"I think what I hear you trying to say is I never dreamed how much I could accomplish."

Lindsey just smiled.

They decided on the way to Lindsey's home that they would call each other every week. And they planned a date for some time in April. This date would be Brady's choice.

At her front door Brady leaned down and kissed Lindsey. She felt his lips warm and soft against hers. She returned his kiss with a longer one. Brady picked her up and walked around in a tiny circle by the door. He set her down and they hugged. Lindsey stepped back and looked up to him and smiled. He came close and kissed her on the top of her head as he whispered, "Dear one" to her. She watched him walk to his SUV. He turned and Lindsey waved to him.

"I love her."

"I love him."

℘

Lindsey slogged her way through the snow, ice and cold of March in Iowa. Everywhere she delivered flowers she heard the words, "Gotta get through this mess of moisture, gotta plant corn, come next month."

And in the first week of April she took her GED and both ACT and SAT tests. One evening Caleb asked her what the GED test was like.

"Glad I studied like I knew I could, the test had five sections, social studies, science, language arts/reading, math, and writing, each with 50 questions, and then a timed essay on a familiar subject."

"Uh huh, and I bet I know what you wrote about, honey bear."

"Yeah, the shop, easiest writing assignment I ever had," she smiled to her uncle. "I know I done good," she looked at him again, "better clean up that grammar," she shook her head, "I did exceedingly well."

She raised her right arm and they high fived.

"Are you seeing Brady again?"

"Yeah, we're having a special date, our Easter date, which we couldn't do at Easter in March because of his field training schedule. It's Brady's choice, and guess what we're doing?"

"Roller skating again?"

"Nope, his mother invited Brady and me and Brady's twin to a noon meal on Sunday, to celebrate Easter late and early birthdays for her sons."

໖

"Lindsey, I'm so pleased to meet you," Darah McDern said as she smiled to Lindsey.

"Nice to meet you ma'am," Lindsey returned as they shook hands. Lindsey looked up at this tall dark-haired and dark-eyed mom.

"Please, call me Darah (rhymes with Sarah)."

"And here's Jared."

"Hi, Lindsey," he shook her hand.

She felt his rock hard callouses, a working man's hand.

Lindsey gasped, "Hi Jared, oh my gosh, how did they tell you apart when you were younger?"

Brady stepped next to his brother.

"Most people couldn't; mom and dad, and a few others, that's all. We played some pretty good jokes on folks back in the day."

Lindsey began to giggle, "Oh my gosh, I bet you did."

All four of them joined in, laughing.

"Oh the stories we could tell."

"Not," Darah spoke out, "you two behave yourselves."

໖

"Can I help you in the kitchen, Darah?"

"Oh yes, we'll leave these two guys to finish setting the table. They have their assigned tasks."

"Sounds like you ran a tight ship when they were younger."

Darah chuckled, "Uh huh, their dad and I did that. We were on the farm then."

In the dining room the brothers split up the table chores.

"Jeez, bro, that little gal looks like she's about 13. She's very pretty, but too short for me."

"Actually she's 16," Brady answered.

"Dude, are you crazy?"

"Wait'll you hear her story, Jared."

₭

"Everything is delicious; I hafta eat my own cooking, or my uncle's so this is a special treat," she smiled to Darah.

"Tell mom and my bro about yourself, Lindsey."

Lindsey explained what she thought Brady's family needed to know about her.

"What year are you in high school?" Darah asked.

"I would be a junior, but I don't go to high school. I just finished up my GED program at Porttown Community College and took my GED. I also prepped for my ACT and SAT's and took those, waiting for all my test results."

Jared asked, "You mentioned you work in a flower shop, do you like floral work?"

"Yeah, I love the work, very labor intensive, and the shop, I own the shop."

"It's none of my business, but I'll ask anyway. How does someone 16 own a flower shop?" Darah wanted to know.

"Sure," Lindsey nodded to her, "with the life insurance money I received after mom's death, I paid off the bank loan on the shop and the shop van. The business is mine, free and clear."

"See what I told you Jared, and mom too, this little lady is special, to her uncle and her friends," Brady gazed at his mom and then at his brother, "and to me."

Lindsey couldn't help herself as she felt a deep blush start at her forehead and move down into her neck. All she managed was to smile to everyone. Brady saw her discomfort and spoke up.

"Didn't mean to make you uncomfortable, Lindsey."

She tried to smile to him, "But you did."

"Let's clear and take our dessert into the living room. Jared started a fire, it's still chilly."

"Yum, Darah, this Black Forest Cake is sublime. I love chocolate."

"Brady told me."

The three of them sipped their coffee and ate cake.

"Bro, when'll you start planting?"

"Dunno," Jared shook his head, "when the soil dries out."

"You're planting corn?" Lindsey asked.

"Right."

"At the shop, that's just about all anyone talks about, getting the corn planted."

"It's a huge deal."

They all nodded.

ഇ

On the drive back to Porttown Lindsey asked, "How did I do with your family? I only felt uncomfortable at the beginning. When your mom invited me to help her, well, helping out, that made me think I'd be OK with her. She's a softer, kinder version of my mom. My mom, her name was Mariah, she was direct, knew exactly what she wanted, not very patient, she really had a mind of her own. Sometimes she didn't know what to do with me."

Brady glanced over to her, "Yeah, 'cause you have a lot of her characteristics, and," he paused, "you did fine with mom and Jared."

Lindsey giggled, "You're right, except I think I'm even more blunt than my mom was. Hey, you didn't talk much about yourself."

She looked over to him as he drove.

"I usually don't have much to say around my mom and brother. Well, dear one, I haven't seen that aspect of you, blunt, but I guess I will."

They drove in silence, glancing at the scenery passing. They saw small signs of spring, the plowed fields, the sides of the roads with tiny chutes of grass poking their heads from the cool soil.

"You're the first young lady I've ever brought home to meet my mom."

"Seriously?"

"Yeah, you surprised her; I know she was happy to meet you. Every mom wants to know who her competition is, what a son of hers is looking for in a woman."

"How do you mean surprised?"

Brady looked across to her as he touched her shoulder, "Your maturity, your initiative, mom was indeed impressed."

"How's your reviewing going for your national and state registries?"

"Good, I study every second I'm not at field training. I think of you, my model of what someone can accomplish. You got through everything, all your testing and running the business. What are you going to do now?"

"Take a week off, at night, to watch all my war DVD's. I'm a WWII movie freak. I don't know why, but I feel sometimes that I've lived another life, before this one, back during that whole war time, in the 1940's. Then I'll read again at night. I used to read five or six books a week. School bored me, but my books, I lived great adventures in my readings. So I'll pile that on. But most important, Uncle Caleb and I will visit the University in Iowa City. We've checked out majors and careers. We're each meeting with an admissions counselor. Now there's a second person interested in the shop. Can you believe it?"

Brady parked in front of her home.

"Yes, I can believe it, from what I see and the little you've told me about how the shop is doing in sales."

"Can you come in?"

He shook his head.

"Wanted to tell you that Uncle Caleb is doing real well, working his physical therapy, almost done with that, seeing his psychologist like he's supposed to. No more suicidal thoughts, sure makes me feel better, no more meds in our home."

Lindsey watched as Brady gave her a big smile.

"I'm so glad, Lindsey, that you don't have that worry, at least not as much, that you feel your uncle's better. Gotta head back to my field training, dear one, I'll have completed all my hours in a month. I have a couple of EMT reserve commitments coming up, will be back in the Bellton area in May. I hope I can see you then."

"I really mean this, Brady, I miss you." Their eyes met as she went on, "You are rock solid, know what you want and are ready to go for it. I feel like you're my mentor. I can tell you about stuff that scares me, that excites me. You excite me, Brady. I see you as a part of my world."

Brady held her hand as they walked up to her front door.

"Dear one," he looked down to her and nodded, "You've been a part of my world since I first laid eyes on you, in your shop, last Christmas."

Lindsey smiled up to him, "Wow, oh wow."

They held each other close. Brady picked her up in a hug and walked around in a little circle with her in his arms. He set her down and leaned down to kiss her.

Lindsey felt his lips, soft, gently plying hers. She felt his tongue as she touched hers to his. A wave of aching moved from her groin up to suffuse her face. They stood together for a time.

"Thank you for the wonderful day, your mom's food, and the opportunity to meet your family, Brady. You're in my prayers, always," she paused, "hoping your studying goes well."

"Accept your thanks, my pleasure, fer sure."

She touched his shoulder, "I love you, Brady, I don't know when that happened, maybe at the accident."

"I love you, Lindsey, we'll talk soon."

Brady watched a smile blossom across her face. She nodded. He kissed her on top of her head. Lindsey gazed at him as he walked back to his car, turned and waved to her. She raised her head, nodded and waved back.

4

Lindsey and Caleb visited Iowa City and the University of Iowa. They talked to admissions counselors. Caleb saw a special counselor for veterans returning from the Iraq and Afghanistan conflicts. Then they had decisions to make. They were both special cases.

Caleb would receive monetary assistance since he earned veterans benefits including his disability situation. He also could apply for other financial aid. And he decided he wanted to look at something in industrial engineering as a major. That's what he did in Afghanistan, worked in villages, helping design and construct schools and hospitals.

Lindsey's situation took a different turn. With the $350,000 pay out on her mom's life insurance policy, Lindsey knew she would not qualify for any kind of aid or scholarship when she attended university. Lindsey kept the payment amount to herself, not saying anything to her uncle or her dad. Jen's dad, a CPA, was both Lindsey's personal and the shop's CPA. Lindsey also asked him to serve as her CFP (Certified Financial Planner), the only other individual who knew of the amount of money Lindsey inherited.

ॐ

"Sheez, now, thinkin' about school, I gotta have help managing my money, not just the shop's," she told Jen when she and Caleb returned from Iowa City.

"My dad, he's helping you with that, right Lindsey?"

"So glad you suggested him to me, Jen, I just didn't know how I wanted to handle the insurance payout, didn't know he was a financial planner, besides being a CPA. You're such a friend, somehow you could see, right after mom died, uh you could just see how overwhelmed I was."

"Hey, Lindsey, I try to put myself in the other guy's shoes; helps me understand how to help."

They hugged as Jen left Lindsey at the shop.

ॐ

April also brought taxes and proms after Lindsey spent a Sunday with Brady and his family.

"Lily, I am so glad I don't have to go to class at night. Between running to the CPA about mom's final personal taxes and the shop's tax situation, I can't believe how busy we are with getting ready for proms. I just didn't realize that we service four different high schools and their proms."

"And, babe, we've got weddings coming up, one almost every Saturday from now to the end of June," Lily smiled to Lindsey.

"All that is great news for us, for the shop," Lily and Lindsey nodded to each other.

And Lindsey accomplished one other thing. After a confirming e-mail from an admissions counselor at Iowa Lindsey applied for admission, not for fall 2005, but for spring 2006. Her admissions counselor suggested she take several classes at Porttown CC as sort of a prep to classes at U. Lindsey found summer school classes, one at 8 a.m. M-W-F and the other at 9 five days a week for eight weeks. The fall class would be 8 a.m. three days a week for the semester. She checked with a transfer evaluator at CC who assured her the three classes, English Comp I, Advanced Spanish, and Chemistry would transfer in to IU. Before Lindsey registered for the summer school classes, she called the admissions counselor at IU, the woman she worked with since Lindsey met her. The counselor checked and got back to Lindsey in a timely fashion.

"Lindsey, I'm happy to report that your transfer folks at your CC are correct. Our transfer evaluators here at IU say those three classes will transfer in and will work with your major. We have a solid working relationship with your CC, try to get as many classes from there as we can to transfer into IU. You know what that means?"

"Yes, Mrs. Brookfield, I'll be ready for rhetoric and a ton of science when I get there in January. And you explained to me that, because of my situation, the College would waive the requirement of a fourth year of a foreign language, if I do good in Advanced Spanish. Besides, I need all the Spanish I can absorb and speak; the Hispanic population is growing fast, everywhere. I'm getting excited to move ahead in my life."

"I'm glad, Lindsey, with your PSAT, ACT, SAT and GED scores, I can pretty much assure you of admission for Spring Semester '06. Our student population declines quite a bit after fall semester. So, you coming in Spring Semester is very good for us. Sounds like you have one hurdle left, your shop."

Mrs. Brookfield knew the goals Lindsey set for herself to enter IU. The shop, finding a buyer for it was Lindsey's challenge.

"That's right, and ma'am, thank you for taking such a personal interest in my situation."

"Yours is pretty unforgettable, 16 years old, following your dreams, one by one."

After the call Mrs. Brookfield spoke out, "Lindsey's mother, wherever you are up there," the counselor raised her eyes to the ceiling, "you must be so proud of your daughter."

ॐ

Brady and Lindsey kept up their weekly phone calls.

"I always want to talk to you, Lindsey, once a week isn't often enough, but for now my studying is going great. I have my registry exams lined up, the first week in June."

"I am so glad to hear you finally have your test dates, Brady, that's awesome to have an end to all this."

"So Lindsey, you're going ahead with your plans to attend IU?"

"I am, gotta be admitted, I have a purpose now, Brady, to work the shop, but I want to do something to help lots more people."

"Well," Brady paused, "you'll certainly do that. And Lindsey, there is something I would like to do for you."

"Ooowww, that sounds, uuummm, uber intriguing."

"Yeah, it's a surprise. I get a Saturday night off from the field internship. Please check your calendar for the second Saturday in May."

"Yeah, I am free, after work, uh any more clues?"

"Right, I'll pick you up at 4:30 at your home. Bring pj's cause Mom is having us stay with her that night. I'll have my old room back and you'll stay in the guest room. You'll be home for church on Sunday 'cause I have to be back at my internship by 2 p.m."

"Wow, Brady, only time I'll be out of town overnight since like forever."

"Oh, did you go to Prom last year as a sophomore?"

"I did."

"Please, wear that dress, uh, what color was it?"

"Light green, sheez Brady, I'm getting excited now, to see you, to be with you, it's been since your birthday celebrations."

"I can't wait to see you."

"Me too, Brady, I have doubts flash before me a lot. Am I doing the right thing, going on to school, ending my mom's dream?"

"Yes, dear one, you are doing the right thing. It'll take you a while to get used to it, but by the time you're a student at the University of Iowa in spring 2006, you'll know it. And, Lindsey, you aren't ending your mom's dream, you're just finishing one of her dreams. You've talked to me about how your mom wanted you to go on to school, and how much you resisted."

"That's right."

"Well, she'll get another dream, your school dream."

"Most of the time my heart tells me I'm doin' the right thing."

"What does God say?"

"Uh huh, He says it's part of His plan for me."

"There you go."

"Take care, I love you, Brady, can't wait to see you, study hard."

"I love you, Lindsey. I know you're thinkin' of me."

"Always."

〜

By the end of the day the last Friday of April Lindsey, Lily and Caleb hugged.

"Was it this nuts last year during prom season?" Caleb asked.

"Yeah, it was, and we got two more Friday and Saturdays to go, just like this one. In these parts Prom is a serious business, something a lot of young people look forward to," Lily said as she stepped back from the two of them.

"Tomorrow may be just as crazy, with mostly guys dropping in for that last minute corsage. We know our stock and what we'll be able to do for customers on short notice," Lindsey gazed at Lily and Caleb and nodded. "And thank you mom," she looked up, "for your notes on how to survive prom time."

"I'm glad, Lindsey, that we'll not be doing any deliveries on the next two Saturdays. It's just too nutsy, getting corsages ready."

ℬ

The craziness repeated itself over the next two Fridays and Saturdays.

"Thank you, Lindsey, for ordering more flowers than we ever have before," Lily exclaimed as she blew out a big breath.

At noon on the second Saturday in May the shop ran out of flowers.

"People must just have money to burn; I know the times are good, but this whole scene is just plain wild," Caleb commented as he looked from Lily to Lindsey.

All three of them had fingers and hands and arms and shoulders that just ached from making all the corsages and boutonnieres. For the next two hours they handed out flowers as young men and women and some adults stopped by.

"Lindsey, get out of here. You have your date coming. Have fun, honey bear and I'll see you tomorrow," Caleb looked at her. "Sheez I feel like a proud dad, sending my daughter off to her?"

"Some kind of special something," Lindsey answered as she came up to him and gave him a hug. Then she hugged Lily.

"We did it, guys, unbelievable, we'll rest good tomorrow 'cause graduation stuff starts before long, Mother's Day, and Memorial Day."

"Oh, this is for you, from Brady."

Caleb handed a corsage box to Lindsey.

She looked at the wrist corsage nestled in the box, raised her eyes to Caleb and Lily, and wept.

∞

"You are beautiful, Lindsey," Brady spoke in a hoarse voice as he stood in the O'Ranon living room. Lindsey heard him try to clear his throat.

"You just do that to me, dear one, kinda take my voice and my breath away."

Brady took her all in, her shining blonde hair, her pale green dress with tiny cap sleeves and demure neckline. They hugged. He moved his head down to kiss her. Their soft lips touched and nuzzled as their tongues went to each other's. They loosened their holds on each other and hugged.

"Have you figured out what's happening, Lindsey?"

"Uh, a dance, Brady, please put my corsage on my wrist. That is so thoughtful of you to get this for me. I didn't make it, had to be Lily or Caleb, doing it and not telling me. It's such a surprise." She paused and looked down for a moment and then back up at him. Tears held in her eyes, "Thank you," she choked out.

Brady took the corsage from its container and slid it on the wrist she offered him. He held her hand and raised it to his lips. He kissed her hand and breathed deep of the fragrance on her wrist.

"Wonderful flowers, wonderful smell," he smiled to her.

Lindsey grabbed her wrap and her overnight bag. Brady took her bag and stayed with her as she dead bolted the front door.

∞

They drove along in silence, noting the plowed fields, already seeded with corn and soybeans and other small grains.

"So, awhile back an old friend, now a teacher, asked me to help chaperone the prom at the high school where she teaches. I promised her I would help out."

Brady looked over to Lindsey and touched her shoulder, "But most importantly I wanted you to have your prom. You never said anything about it, knowing that you were leaving high school. But girls told me over the years that the prom is something a young woman looks so forward to, like her wedding day."

"Wow Brady, this will be a wonderful time for me, I sure need a special time, a break away."

"Good for you, I'm happy to help make that time wonderful. I want to be with you, Lindsey, now and always."

๛

Many young couples sat around them as they ate dinner in the nice restaurant. Lindsey admired the girls in their pretty dresses, and lots of the young men wore tuxedoes.

"This is my first time seeing you in a suit, you look so," she paused, "handsome." She smiled to Brady from across the table.

"Thanks Lindsey, this is my first time seeing you in a dress."

"All I can say is that I'm not sure I'd recognize us, the way we're dressed now, that is, if I just was passing by."

Brady chuckled, "Do we look that different?"

Lindsey gave a deep nod to her head, "Uh huh."

After they ate, they decided to wait on dessert until after the dance.

๛

Lindsey looked up at the lavender and blue crepe paper crisscrossing the entire gym ceiling. Balloons and netting set along the pushed back gym seats added to the lavender and aqua colors.

"Gosh, the students, the juniors, they did a nice job, Valerie."

Valerie nodded to Lindsey, "Right, they worked really hard to make this a special dance for the seniors. At first they wanted to do this prom in a hotel meeting room in Bellton, but after checking the situation out, they decided on the gym. It's a lot bigger. And they saved a bunch on rent."

Brady introduced Lindsey to Valerie a few minutes earlier. Brady and Valerie went to school together in eighth and ninth grades. Valerie moved away, but they stayed in touch with each other over the years. Now she worked with Bellton High School students as a math teacher. She needed chaperones, and Brady offered to help out.

"We've been friends for a long time, Lindsey. Brady, he's just a super guy," she smiled and nodded as she looked from Brady to Lindsey.

"Is this anything like your Senior Prom?" Valerie asked.

Lindsey turned to Valerie as her voice wavered, "I, I didn't have a prom, except last year, as a sophomore. This is the dress I wore then."

"Oh, gosh."

"This night is a special date night, a surprise," Brady said.

Lindsey looked from Brady to Valerie, "He's so, so kind. Valerie, this is my Prom."

Valerie gazed at Lindsey, "Brady is a special guy, always has been." She shifted her gaze to him, "I'm so happy he's doing this for you, and helping me chaperone too."

The two women smiled to each other. Valerie gave them brief instructions for chaperoning.

"Mostly you two should dance and have fun."

Lindsey held on to his hand as he got ready to turn her, and turn her. They danced and danced.

"Having fun?" Brady's dark eyes sparkled into hers.

"Yeah, so awesome, you are such a strong lead, sometimes I think I'm gonna fly up off the floor," she laughed.

They held hands as they found a place to stand and drink their punch behind the crowds of dancing students.

A slow song came on and they danced close. Lindsey turned her head and rested it on his wide chest. He kissed her on top of her head as the song concluded. Several Bellton High faculty walked up to Brady through the evening. He introduced his former teachers to Lindsey. They thanked Brady for his EMT service to the communities he served.

"Hey, I always knew Brady would do something in medical. He was by my side whenever we had a medical emergency, whether it was on the football field, or the basketball court, or out on the track."

When he left, Brady explained that Coach Borders was either his head or assistant head coach in all the sports in which Brady participated.

"Working with injuries, I knew where I was headed, Lindsey," Brady nodded to her as his eyes pooled into hers.

Lindsey looked up to him, "He helped inspire you, Brady."

Brady nodded to her and held her by her shoulders, close to him. "He did, he and quite a few others folks, too."

They danced every dance, the rest of the night.

"It was magic, Brady, my prom, it was magic. I had so much fun with you."

They held hands as they walked out of the gym to his SUV.

She turned to him after he opened her door, "You are so kind to me, somehow knowing what I needed, even though I didn't know it myself. Thank you."

She put her arms around him as he held her close. Tears streamed down her face.

She struggled for a little while, then looked up to him, "Brady, these are happy tears, I'm, I'm just overwhelmed right now."

∽

They found a little café that remained open late. Brady sat across from Lindsey as they ate warm cherry pie with vanilla ice cream.

"Brady, I'm putting my brain around the next couple of years. I'm praying that your studying goes well, that God has your plan, you'll find that job." Lindsey paused, "Paramedic, yeah, my dream, my hope for you."

Brady watched her smile and nod as she spoke, "I have a goal, but mine's several years away. Yours is immediate."

"That's why we need to have this conversation, Lindsey. You won't have your final year of high school, going straight on to a university setting. I really feel you missed a chunk of your teenage years."

She looked him in the eye, "Right, working a lot in the shop since I was 13. So you are getting at?"

"Getting at the fact that you need to meet people, have fun, especially when you get to the U of I, you'll live in the dorm spring semester?"

"Uh huh, university requirement, for that semester, plus Uncle Caleb insists on it, like you he wants me to have that freshman experience."

"What's Caleb's situation?"

Brady watched her give him a wide smile, "He heard, he's admitted for Fall Semester, but he's gonna defer until spring, to help us in the shop plus he's my guardian. When he goes to IU, he'll get a place, two bedrooms. I'll help him with his rent. The plan is for me to live with him for a year, starting the summer after my semester in the dorm. Then I'll be on my own, a big kid, 18."

"Sounds like your plan is coming together," Brady took her hand from the table and held it in his own, "as I said I want a job somewhere in a 60 mile radius of Iowa City."

"I remember that conversation, Brady. If you do get a job in the area, maybe we will get to see each other, I would really like that."

"Me too, after my tests in June, then I'm full bore into findin' that job."

They left the restaurant and stopped in front of his mom's home.

"Brady, can we walk for a little bit? The star-studded sky makes me want to be out under its canopy."

They held hands as they walked along.

"How, how, Brady, can I thank you for your kindnesses to me, my prom, I never even thought of it, meeting your family, I would have never guessed I'd get to do that. I feel so fortunate to have you in my life."

She moved her head, looking up to him.

He stopped her and turned to her, "Keep on doing what you're doing, you told me you pray for me, please continue."

They smiled to each other, hugged and walked back to the front door. Before they went in, Brady bent down and kissed her as she rose up on her toes to meet his kiss. Lindsey felt a heat rise from her groin up to her forehead. Brady felt an urgent heat of his own.

At the kitchen table they sat, sipping warm milk and eating the oatmeal raisin cookies Brady's mom left out for them.

"My favorite," he held up the cookie he was about to consume.

"Mental note, Lindsey," she said out loud, "he likes oatmeal raisin."

They smiled to each other. Brady saw her tired eyes.

"To bed, sweet dreams, Lindsey."

He hugged her and she replied, "Wake up bright in the morning light. That was mom's saying to me at night after we stopped saying prayers together."

Instant tears came to her eyes as they separated.

"Time, Lindsey, time will heal you."

She wiped her tear-filled eyes with her hands and tried to smile, "I hope, soon."

Brady and Lindsey spoke words of encouragement to each other as they parted that Sunday morning.

℘

"Lily, I read mom's notes about graduations, Mother's Day and Memorial Day. Time's just goin' by so fast."

"Yeah, Lindsey, last year was busy. Since our shop services three other small towns plus Porttown, we order up twice the number of flower in each of our deliveries. Times are good. Folks don't seem to mind paying for fresh flowers for their loved ones graves."

Lindsey walked up to Lily and began shaking her head.

"Lily, Caleb and me, uh, we still haven't figured out what to do with mom's ashes."

Lily hugged Lindsey as they both began to cry, "It'll come to you, babe, when the time is right. Remember that the mortuary will keep the cremains until you decide."

Almost every day of the week before Memorial Day, Caleb and Lindsey delivered flowers to God's Gardens, the graveyard on the edge of Porttown. They followed the accurate legend which explained where the graves were located.

"Caleb, are you as tired as I am?"

It was Friday afternoon, and they put the last set of flowers on the last grave for that day.

"Like I say, Lindsey, this whole business is very labor intensive."

He walked next to her as they headed back to the shop van.

"But you know what, I feel like the folks in the graves, like they're standing next to us as we put the flowers on their graves. It's weird, to me they're all still with us, just in a form which is above our ability to see them or to hear them."

Lindsey touched his arm and he turned to her, "Uncle Caleb, I feel that all the time about mom, that's she right with me. I don't feel that here at God's Garden, not yet, think I have to be older."

Lindsey looked up to him, "And it's you too, you remind me so much of mom, same hazel eyes, same sandy blonde hair."

℘

"Well, I'm glad I work full time. That makes it easier to understand about how many hours going to school takes, how much effort goes into the homework and the getting ready for tests," Lindsey told Brady as they spoke on the phone.

"I'll know soon, Lindsey, about my test scores. I feel good about how I did. How are comp and Spanish?"

"Brutal, glad I have a good work ethic, or this summer'll kill me. Some nights I have five hours of homework. But it's only for a few more weeks and then I get two weeks for a break before my chemistry class starts."

The phone remained quiet for a few seconds.

"Lindsey?"

"Yeah, I'm here, Brady."

"I'm so busted for money. I've applied for a couple of paramedic positions, but there are plenty of applicants. There're more openings for the EMT area. I'll take an EMT job in the right location. I gotta start making money. My student loan money is gone, and I must work and start to pay the loan back. My bro even asked me to come home to help out on the farm. I'd rather wash dishes in a café than do that kind of work again."

"It's all going to come together, Brady, it's tough to get started. Maybe do EMT for a year and ease into a paramedic situation then."

"You're right, I must find work. So I'm kinda down right now. You are so busy with work and school."

"I keep you in my prayers, Brady, always."

"Thank you, keep doing that."

"I feel helpless, God, help Brady," Lindsey whispered after she hung up the phone.

She thought for a little bit.

"I know what I have to do, my best, at work and at school. That's what will help Brady the most. I got his back; he's got mine. That's our situation now," she spoke the words out loud.

ℰↃ

Every week during all of June and early July Lily, Caleb and Lindsey prepared flowers for weddings in Porttown and small towns nearby.

"I love the Saturday weddings," she commented to Lily as they drove to a church on the outskirts of Porttown.

"My favorites too, Lindsey, I been toying with the idea of taking a class or two at CC, event planning kind of stuff, and I bought a book about wedding planning. I'd like to do that class and get certified as a wedding planner. That might boost our bottom line and get me some advanced experience."

Lindsey took her eyes from the road for a moment and looked over to Lily.

"Wow, that's such a great idea; we really do a lot of wedding planning with each wedding event that we do. That will really help you, Lily, if you decide to go on and do more advanced work."

Lindsey pulled the van up to the side of the church, to the door the minister wanted them to use. In two hours she and Lily transformed the church into a wonderland of pink and red flowers, chosen by the bride. Flowers clung to the sides of the pews and along both sides of the steps leading up to the altar. They moved to the fellowship hall across from the church sanctuary and put floral decorations on all pale pink table-clothed circular tables. They placed a long and narrow pink and red floral display in front of the bride and groom's places at their special table. The shop's final box Lily brought in were all the flowers for the bride, groom, attendants and parents of the bride and groom.

Lily and Lindsey stood next to each other as they took one final look around at the church and the reception area.

"We do beautiful work, Lindsey," Lily smiled and caught Lindsey's eye.

"Yes, we do, thanks for all you do, Lily. You've taken the pictures you want?"

"Uh huh, we're getting such a nice album of weddings we've done last summer through the year and now. It gives brides and grooms more ideas about what they might want."

Lindsey hugged Lily, "Someday this may be us, when we find that loved one."

They stepped back from each other and looked each other in the eye.

"We'll sure as heck know what to do," Lily chuckled, and Lindsey joined in with her laugh.

∽

"It's so good to see you, Lindsey."

Lindsey came up to Brady as he sat in a chair on the back patio. She bent down behind his chair, put her arms around his shoulders, and hugged him as she placed her cheek next to his.

"Thanks for coming, Brady on this grand Fourth of July, I wanta hear your news and then have our picnic with Caleb and Lily. It was super hard for me to study this morning, imagining what you'd have to say."

"So you didn't go to church."

"Nope, I had to get my five hours study in for classes tomorrow morning. Only four more weeks and then I get a break before chem starts. But I sorta liked chemistry in high school. This shouldn't be much different, what'll I do with all my spare time, duh, just one class to study for?"

Brady smiled to her, "No fear, you'll fill the time, maybe volunteer?"

"Stop, I gotta hear what you have to say," Lindsey said.

Brady watched her clutch her coffee cup. He saw her knuckles go white.

"Well, for starters, it's a miracle I got today off, but I did. I have to be back for my shift starting at midnight."

"I've been calling you on your cell phone. I don't know where you live, or anything."

Lindsey shook her head as she poured him more lemonade.

"I passed my registries. I'm a for real paramedic."

Lindsey watched a smile widen across his face as his dark eyes sparked across to hers.

"Oh, wow," Lindsey paused, "just like that you tell me, so calm, so matter of fact, congratulations Brady."

She unclenched her hands from her coffee cup and took one last swig. Lindsey reached across the table to shake his right hand.

"Tell me more."

Brady shifted in his chair. Lindsey watched his solemn face and his lips thin in concentration.

"I don't have a paramedic job; I've applied for positions in three different locations. But," he shook his head, "no job. They all told me to keep checking back and looking on line; that's where most locations post."

He scooted back his chair to give him more room.

"I got various advice from guys in the field. They suggested for me not to take an EMT position which I know I could get right now. I'd have to leave it if something opened up for a paramedic and I got the job. That might not look too good on my medical resume. They suggested I look at a long term EMT reserve slot. It could be most anywhere in the state, but since it's reserve, I could walk away without it hurting me too much, wouldn't look like I was job hopping."

Lindsey smiled to him and nodded, "Makes sense, reserves go where they are needed, it's an immediate need, you're filling in, right?"

"Uh huh, you got it."

"You got a reserve slot, right?"

"I do have, the one I'm on now ends tomorrow morning. I start my new one on Tuesday, but it's up in the north part of the state, and it's five months, 'til early December. They need me in that district; they plan to bring someone on board after me. But they want time to recruit and hire an EMT. Right now, there's an imbalance in some places in the state, more paramedics and fewer EMT's."

Brady watched Lindsey furrow her brow and look him in the eyes, "Is that an imbalance that can be cleared up, more EMT's soon?"

"Right, it happens from time to time, I feel that the right paramedic position will pop up. For now I gotta have employment wherever I can get it."

"Do you have a place to live?"

"In Sankville, with two other paramedics in the district, they got a house with an extra bedroom. I'll get to use the kitchen. I drove up there, met them on duty, they gave me a house key and said they'd be glad to have help with the rent. So I'm set for the next five months." He looked across to Lindsey, "And it'll be great experience, working with paramedics, I'll essentially do what they do."

"One day at a time, Brady," Lindsey spoke out as she nodded.

"That's for sure."

They stood up together. Brady came around and hugged Lindsey. Then he picked her up and walked around in a circle.

"I'm so proud of you, Brady," she whispered in his ear. "Your dream, it's unfolding right before our eyes."

He set her down gently. She looked up into his eyes.

"My love for you is strong; it'll hold us through these long days and months when we can't be together," Lindsey said as Brady saw tears fill her eyes.

He nodded, "Strong, so strong, that's my love for you, Lindsey you light my world with love."

He bent down and touched his lips to hers. She felt his tongue teasing hers and touched his tongue back. Lindsey felt an urgent spasm in her groin. They held their kiss for a time. Brady lifted his lips from hers and looked down to her.

"Time, Lindsey, time is what we must have, to see if this passion for each other is real, for all time, or just a passing phase."

෨

They chowed down on fried chicken Lily brought, potato salad Brady picked up at the store and corn on the cob, Lindsey's contribution. Caleb provided pop and ice cream cake. They sat around the patio table and laughed at the story Caleb just finished telling about the young Afghan children and their reactions on their first day of school. This was a school Caleb and his Army troops built after the children's old school got destroyed by incoming mortar fire months before.

"I must leave. I want you to go to the fireworks with Caleb and Lily. You've got so much ahead of you, Lindsey, years of education, I've just got to find that job that fits me."

"I'm so glad you came and told me your plans in person."

"Thanks for the picnic; delicious chow, my first meal in your home, Lindsey."

She held his hand as they walked to his SUV.

"There'll be many more to come, more meals, Brady, you and me, together."

They kissed and held on tight.

"Safe travels, God speed," she said as she backed away from him.

She waved as he got into his SUV. She saw his wave back as he began to drive away.

5

Lindsey hung up the cell phone.

"Thank you for your call; God, thank you for Brady calling me. I am so happy after his calls, thank you, oh thank you," she spoke out as she whirled around the small kitchen.

She grabbed coffee and walked back to her bedroom. She concentrated best when she sat on the floor with her books and papers around her. She plopped down and found her last chemistry test. It had a red A on the front.

"Unbelievable, I do A work, I really can do A work, just have to apply myself," she whispered.

Halloween fast approached. The shop was busy with Homecoming just the week before. And Saturday they had the wedding flowers for a wedding in Porttown. Lindsey figured she had two hours of homework every night after she got home from work. She liked that a lot better than the load she carried during summer school. She worked through her chemistry problems and finished her homework and reading for tomorrow. Some nights now Lindsey was home alone until about her bedtime. Caleb spent evenings with Lily at her place. Lindsey felt happy for them. She went back to the kitchen. She took the letter with her that she did not open for several days.

"I'm afraid it's stuff about Crystal and grandma; I'm not sure I can face that," she kept telling herself.

"It's now or never."

She noted the return address, a particular law office in Ames. She opened the envelope with care. Lindsey felt the tears begin, stinging her eyes as leaned against the kitchen counter, reading through the information. She was unable to finish the reading. She stood in the middle of the kitchen with the letter in one hand and a paper towel in the other to mop up her runny nose and wet face.

Lindsey read and reread the letter, comprehending the information. She sat down at the kitchen table, grabbed a yellow highlighter and marked information in the letter. She heard the garage door open. Caleb put his pickup in and closed the garage door. As he came in the door to the kitchen, Lindsey spoke up.

"Uncle Caleb, there's this letter I got. You need to read it."

Caleb smiled as he sat down across from Lindsey. He took a sip of the coffee he just poured for himself. He read the letter once, then twice more. Lindsey wrote down a couple of notes from what she remembered reading.

"Wow, Lindsey, your mom, she's really incredible."

"She is."

"Honey bear, please look at me."

Lindsey gazed across at her uncle.

"What do you want to do about this request?"

Caleb and Lindsey talked together for about 15 minutes and made a decision.

"We'll pick the time, and I think this couple should come to the shop, to see where Mariah worked, to see what her world was like."

"Mom goes on," Lindsey added.

"Yes, she does," Caleb nodded in agreement.

ℰ◌

Ten days before Thanksgiving Lindsey met with her lawyer. He approved of the contract Lindsey and the bank had for the sale of her flower shop.

"Mr. Frampton, I can't believe it, looks like I really am going to IU."

He watched her eyes brighten up as she said that.

"All that's left is the loan approval for the buyers. Looks like you'll have a little money set aside for your future education, or whatever your plans are."

Her lawyer smiled to her, "You're sure you want to wait to turn over the shop until the first of the year?"

"Absolutely, we need this Christmas season to bring up our revenue to where I'd like it to be. Besides, Mrs. Clarkley is going to come in to the store for the last three weeks of December. She wants us to teach her the business. The only way to learn is to be there in the daily operations. Lily is staying on, at least for a while, to assist her. She's getting a nice raise from the new owner too."

"Smart move on the part of the new owner," she watched her lawyer nod his head in approval.

ℰ◌

"I'm on duty 10 days in a row this Thanksgiving holiday," Brady spoke to her on his cell.

"Gosh, hope you'll get to have a turkey dinner, Brady."

Brady laughed into the phone, "Yeah, at the firehouse, the food is tasty there."

"I'm missing you like crazy, four months, it's been."

"The Fourth of July, I still have the day memorized in my mind, Lindsey, seeing you, having a meal with you, spending time with you and Caleb and Lily."

"Chemistry's great; didn't realize how much I like science, guess I always did, but I just didn't get it, at the time."

"That sounds like a fer sure A."

"Uh huh, and I have news, unbelievable news."

"Talk to me, dear one."

She heard the gentle tone of his voice as she felt hot tears erupt in her eyes.

"Uh, I'm gonna cry a little."

"Just go slow."

"I'll back up."

Brady heard her breathe in and out. "Mom, she talked to Uncle Caleb years ago about having her organs donated if anything ever happened. Uh, in the accident her spine got severed, but everything else made her a case for organ donation."

"Wow, I didn't know that."

"Anyhow, two days ago we had a special couple come into the shop at 10 a.m. They introduced themselves to Uncle Caleb and me. Then the lady burst into tears. Her husband tried to calm her down, but she cried and cried. We had them sit down at the table where we help customers with floral requests."

"Lindsey, who's the lady?"

"Her name is Diana McPhersal. She has my mom's heart, beating right in her chest. She didn't think she even would still be alive for this holiday season. But Diana's doing fine, thanks to my mom's strong heart."

"She thanked me, and Uncle Caleb, for mom saving her life."

Lindsey began crying into the phone. When she calmed down she spoke again, "I got up and went to her; she stood up and we hugged and hugged. I kept saying mom, mom you're still alive through Diana. It's a miracle."

Then Diana and I broke down and cried again. She and her husband took Uncle Caleb and me out to lunch, down at the little café where we had our first meal. We had a grand visit together. She told us her unbelievable story, her struggles, and we shared a little about our lives. I showed the couple the picture I keep of mom. After lunch I asked them to come back to the shop with us. Earlier I fixed up an arrangement of flowers for Diana to take with her. When I gave the flowers to her I told her, "Mom loved daisies and roses and carnations, pink was mom's favorite color."

"So, most of the flowers were pink, right Lindsey?" Brady asked.

"Uh huh, I, I am just so sad, right now, mom helped folks, she did."

"Lindsey, I go in for a second interview, a paramedic job, outside Iowa City, I want it."

"Brady, I have so much faith in you; my heart tells me this is a good situation for you, yeah, a good feeling."

"God is with me, Lindsey, every step of the way."

"Yes He is. He watches over you and me, you with your crazy hours and all the traveling you are doing between the north and east parts of our state."

"Keep me in your prayers, Lindsey, I love you. I know you have so much going on, finishing chem, the sale of the shop, getting set for school, you're almost a college student, how does that feel?"

"Scary."

"We'll talk; you're in my thoughts."

"You're in mine, Brady, I love you."

ॐ

"What in the name of heck are we gonna do with all our stuff, Uncle Caleb?" Lindsey asked as they stood together in the middle of their living room.

"Sell it, give it away. I want my box springs and mattress. I bought them after I moved in with you and sis; I'll haul them to my next place."

"Massive garage sale?" she asked as she looked over to her uncle.

"Yeah, plus right now you know you can't take anything but personal stuff and clothes, beings you'll be in the dorm."

"Right, you can take more stuff, to set up your apartment."

"We've done it, Lily."

Lily watched as a smiling Lindsey walked up to her. Lily stood in the discarded flowers and greenery all over the floor around her and the work table.

"Good for you, Lindsey, you got Caleb all packed?"

"Yup, he's on his way to Iowa City; he's so excited to get his place and get set up for his semester."

"What about you?"

"Our rental, it's all cleaned, sleeping on an air mattress borrowed from a neighbor until I move out on Christmas Eve. I'm staying with Jen from Christmas Day until I leave on the first, then it'll be at Caleb's until the dorm opens up, just a couple of days."

"How're you feeling about all the change, Lindsey?"

Lindsey sat down in a chair and propped her chin with her hand. She thought for a moment, "I'm just trying to keep my days and tasks straight, kinda like after mom died, puttin' one foot in front of the other."

Lily came to her and patted her shoulder as she leaned down to catch Lindsey's eyes.

"You're doing terrific, babe, and I am proud of you."

"Thanks, Lily, for your kind words." Tears came to Lindsey's eyes, "Sometimes I'm not sure I'm doing the right thing. Oh my gosh, Lily, this shop's been my whole life for a year, wow," she paused, "no, longer than that."

Lindsey watched Lily nod her head and smile to her.

&

Jill Clarkley came in at 11:30 the Monday of Christmas week. Lindsey ordered pizza for the three of them. They discussed how well the shop was doing this holiday season as they sat in the back area eating and having coffee.

"We have a whole week of business, including Christmas Eve, this Saturday." Lindsey nodded as she looked from Lily to Jill. "Like last year, folks seem to want to spend money on flowers for loved ones."

"You two are such good teachers; I guess I didn't realize how labor intensive the work is. My shoulders and hands and feet, those first few days, I'm doing better now," Jill smiled to them. "Lily, I'm so glad you're staying on, for a while."

Lily looked over to Jill and nodded, "Just like with Lindsey last Christmas, this is my job, Jill."

"Oh, ladies, I also want to thank you for sending out the business Christmas cards about the transfer of ownership of the shop."

"Jill, that information, names and addresses, is in the master notebook in the December section. I remember mom suggesting sending cards a couple years ago, but she didn't follow through. Both Lily and I can name off our best customers in a quick minute. Now you'll know, as you come forward to take over. These are folks you can count on for business, at least for now in these good times."

"That's wonderful news, Lindsey."

"And Jill," Lindsey paused, "we're glad you're keeping the same name for the shop. People know us by that name and our reputation for quality service and flower products will keep people coming back to buy from you."

"Want to talk about the website?"

"It'll stay the same for now, Lily. Internet connectivity is still a work in progress in our area of Iowa. The good old telephone plus our internet connection for teledelivery is the way I want to progress. Lindsey, will you help at the shop next Tuesday while Lily and I get the church ready for the evening wedding?"

"I will, basically I'm in the shop through a week from Saturday." As Lindsey went about her tasks that day she kept repeating a prayer to herself, "You are making this happen, God. I thank you for the good people I work with."

ɶ

"Happy Birthday to me, happy birthday to me," Lindsey sang out as she made coffee that morning. Just as she headed for her shower with her coffee cup in hand she heard the home phone ring. She tracked back to the kitchen.

Brady sang the birthday song to her. She joined in and a duet began.

"And many more," Brady sang by himself.

"How's my very growed up gal of seventeen?" he drawled.

"Dude, right now I feel a whole lot older than that."

"Everthin' all right there?"

"Yes Brady, and thank you for remembering my day. Are you on the road?"

"Yeah, can't talk but a minute 'cept to tell you I took a paramedic position."

"Thank you God, for bringing Brady and this job together."

"I knew you'd want to know; just you and mom for right now."

"Congratulations!"

"You're headin' out, the first?"

"That's it; you got my cell number, right Brady?"

"I do, so much happening, I know you're busy as heck at the shop. We'll celebrate your birthday, and Christmas and New Year's, all together, when we see each other."

"Brady, I love you, but take your time, your new job, let's plan on seeing each other once I'm in the dorm, maybe after classes start. Gosh, my mind's spinnin' with," she stopped, unable to talk.

"I understand, I love you, Lindsey, you're first, in my thoughts, and in my prayers."

Lindsey heard the tone of his soft voice, that same voice he always spoke to her with, his care and concern.

"God speed and good luck, Brady."

"Take care, Lindsey."

Lindsey cried as she showered. Her thoughts went to her mom. As she headed out the door of the nearly empty house, it finally came to her that this part of her life was near its end.

"I'll do deliveries. Jill, is that OK? I need to stop at one special place. Somethin' I need to do as a thank you."

Jill nodded and smiled to Lindsey. Lindsey left the shop with the afternoon deliveries on that Thursday afternoon before Christmas on Sunday. She wheeled into the delivery spot near the fire station. She walked in with her The Flower Shop jacket on. Lindsey created the arrangement she held, with red roses, and white carnations and small bits of Douglas fir greenery for Joe. Lindsey attached the envelope and card inside with a plastic fastener.

She told the fireman who greeted her inside that she had a delivery for Joe.

"There is just one Joe at this fire station, right?"

The fireman who appeared so tall and broad smiled down to her.

"Yes, Miss, there's just one Joe. He's having lunch with the rest of us. I'll let you talk to him."

"Sure it's OK? I don't want to interrupt."

"No worries, please come with me."

Lindsey sat in a small reception area. As Joe approached, Lindsey stood with the floral arrangement in her hands.

"The, the, this is for you, Joe, from me."

Lindsey did not really remember his face as he smiled to her. He held the arrangement and bent his head down to smell the roses.

"Ah, roses, so wonderful," he said as he lifted his head and looked at her.

"Please, let's sit."

"Uh, uh, read the note in the envelope, it'll help you."

He set the arrangement on the table and opened the envelope.

Joe, My Uncle Caleb was in his bedroom being revived from a drug overdose. You're the kind fireman who led me out of his room and took me to the kitchen. Thanks for helping me mop up from all my crying. My mom had died a little before at Christmas and having that happen to Uncle Caleb, it was the worst day of my life. I don't remember what you said to me, but just your being there, that saved me and my life got better from that day forward. Lindsey

Tears filled Lindsey's eyes as he looked up from his reading and gazed at her.

"What now, for you, Lindsey?"

"I'm headed to the University of Iowa, student in the College of Nursing."

"And then?"

"Take care of folks, like you took care of me, thanks for what you do, Joe, I have to head back to the shop."

Lindsey stood. Joe saw her jacket with the shop name on it. She held out her hand as he got up. They shook hands. She felt the rock-hard surface of the inside of his hand. Lindsey smiled her biggest smile to him. He nodded to her and gave her a small wave. Lindsey hurried from the fire station.

She blew out a big breath and spoke out, "Thank you, all you folks who will continue to guide and protect me."

Lindsey returned to the shop but decided not to share her visit to the fire station with Lily and Jill. On Christmas Eve afternoon, a Saturday, she helped close the shop. Lily, Lindsey, and Jill stood outside looking at the shop as customers saw it. They hugged each other and wished each other Merry Christmas.

Lindsey felt the sun disappear under a cloud as she drove into the driveway of the home she lived in these past few years. She got out and looked at the neatly shoveled walk she worked on early in the day.

"More snow, I wonder," she spoke out as she unlocked the door. She looked through the house, making sure she had not left anything. The new renters would move in the day after Christmas.

"There was a lot of love here," she hollered out and heard her echo. She hauled the necessary items for her semester from near the front door to her car. "I hope there will continue to be love in this home," she spoke in a quieter tone as she locked the front door from the inside. Lindsey left her house key on the kitchen counter for the landlord. She felt a flood of emotion and tears came as she backed out of the driveway.

"Are you sure you know what you're doing, Lindsey?" she asked herself. As she drove to Jen's, a warmth settled around her.

"Is that you, God?" she smiled to herself and nodded.

℘

Lindsey settled in to the guest bedroom. Jen helped her bring what she would need for her stay until New Year's Day.

Jen and Lindsey sat on Lindsey's bed.

"I just feel shaky as heck, scared, leaving my home, going away to school. I was so sure of myself until a day or so ago."

Jen hugged her, "Babe, I think that's normal, I think that'll happen to me when I head to State in the fall. Don't want to baby you, Lindsey, but you just turned 17, and that's a little younger than most kids are when they head out. Hey," she paused and looked into Lindsey's eyes, "take it easy, you're with me for a week, we can hang out. You go back to work on Monday, your last week at the shop, like you promised Jill, right?"

"Uh huh, glad you understand about my being unsettled."

"Just enjoy being here, with me and my folks."

That evening Brady called her. He was on a break and he knew he would head out soon.

"Brady, I took flowers to a fireman, Joe. He spent time with me after I discovered Uncle Caleb, when he dang near died."

"What did you give Joe?"

"Pretty much the bouquet you decided on for your mom, that Christmas week a year ago, lemmesee, red roses, which Joe liked, white carnations and the bits of evergreen. I wrote him a note 'cause I knew I wouldn't be able to talk to him about Uncle Caleb. He thanked me. That made me feel so good."

"You feel better when you give than when you receive, Lindsey."

"You're right about that; I don't accept gifts very well."

"Uh, neither do I, that's why I asked that we not give each other gifts for the holidays. Your gift to me is your love, Lindsey."

"Same for you, Brady."

§つ

Uncle Caleb also called wishing her a happy Christmas. He got settled into his new place and even bought a tiny Christmas tree. He said he would leave it up for Lindsey when she arrived. He knew the only Christmas tree she would see was at Jen's.

"I loved midnight mass," Lindsey shared with Jen and her parents as they drove home.

"Lindsey, while we're all together in the car, well, I mentioned this to you at the end of our last session of my being your CPA. Should you ever want to return to Porttown, you are always welcome in our home. Jen doesn't have to be here; we consider you like a second daughter."

Lindsey burst into tears. When she could speak it out, she thanked the three of them for taking care of her.

"A place to come home to, that will be so wonderful," she hugged Jen as they sat in the backseat of the car.

☙

Christmas Day passed, and Lindsey ached for her mom. She felt relieved to go back to the shop. Time passed quicker there.

☙

"Do you want some help unpacking your car at the dorm, Lindsey?"

"No thanks, Uncle Caleb. This is my deal. I'm excited to get going with my new life, and I appreciate you letting me stay with you until my dorm opened."

"Well, maybe I'll see you at the bookstore, or I can come visit you at your dorm."

Lindsey stood in front of her uncle.

"Where would I be if it weren't for you, Uncle Caleb?"

"I dunno, honey bear. But I've sure enjoyed you growing up these last few months."

"Not the brat I once was."

"That's fer sure, come 'ere, I need a hug."

Lindsey stepped to him and they hugged. As she let go, tears came to her eyes.

"I am," she sobbed, "very grateful for you being in my life, dear uncle."

Caleb wiped a tear that rolled down his cheek, "It's been my pleasure."

6

"Mind if I join you?" Lindsey asked as she stood across from the blonde, blue-eyed young man with brown-framed glasses. "I saw you at breakfast yesterday, and you were alone then."

"Please do, I appreciate the company, you gotta be a morning person like me, have ta have breakfast."

"That's for sure, I'm Lindsey."

She held out her hand to him and they shook.

"Jacob."

"The food here is so good; I been doing my own cooking for a while."

They ate together in silence.

"More milk?"

"Not for me, but I would take a cup of coffee, black."

"I'm on it."

Lindsey brought back two cups of coffee.

"Love this stuff," she nodded to him, "just started drinking it about a year ago."

"What you studying, Lindsey?"

"Nursing."

"Yer kiddin' me, that's my field."

Lindsey watched a big smile appear on his face.

"I thought I saw someone who looked like you in Anatomy yesterday."

"Yeah, I saw you too, what I noticed was how young you looked."

She nodded to him and smiled, "It's my size, just turned 17, holy crud, Jacob," she stopped for a second, "are you in Micro and 1030 Nursing?"

"I am."

"This is my first semester at IU; I took CC classes last summer and fall."

"Well, this is my first semester back. I started Fall 2004, but got terrible sick, barely finished the semester, had a kidney transplant at Christmas and was advised to take a year off. I did, now feeling good, actually, the docs say it's a miracle I lived."

"It was good to meet you, Jacob. Take care of yourself, the workload'll be intense."

"See you," he smiled to her as she picked up her dishes.

"Nice guy, I'll see him in some of my classes," she spoke out as she headed back to her dorm room to figure out the rest of her classroom locations.

&

A week went by. After her first Saturday of studying all day Lindsey made a decision. She called the University of Iowa's Medical Center volunteer office and inquired about volunteering somewhere in the Center on Saturday mornings. She needed a break from the constant studying. Back in her old life she had a variety of activities, working at the shop six days a week, being with Jen when she could, night classes and studying and keeping a home. Her life was busier then. Now all she had to do was eat and sleep and study. The roommate she was supposed to have did not materialize. The girl's parents came one day and took away the possessions the girl left over the holidays. She decided she would not return to IU.

Lindsey missed Porttown; she had a good case of homesickness. At night, when she tried to settle down to sleep, that's when it hit her hardest. Her mom continued to loom in her mind, and the flowers, she missed the smells and the creations she accomplished. She missed tending her flowers.

℘

"I'm looking at your volunteer application and your referrals, Lindsey. How would you like to train to work as a volunteer in the ER for three hours on Saturday mornings?" Samantha Griffith asked in her call to Lindsey.

"Yes, Saturday morning, I'd be interested in that."

"We'll get your TB tests done and your background check, you'll work with an ER trainer, and we need you, Lindsey, uh, you know what Saturday mornings are like, right?"

"Uh huh, spillover from Friday nights of boozing and shooting up, fight clean ups, lots of stitches."

"You are so on target, you must have asked around."

Actually, Lindsey had. She and Jacob continued to have breakfast together in the dorm dining hall. And they started meeting at the library to study from 6:30 to 11 p.m. Sunday through Thursday. Jacob worked for three hours on Friday nights, his volunteer shift at the IU Med Center. He already saw quite a repertoire of ailments and situations that came through the doors of the ER since he started in early January. He volunteered at the ER a year before, in the fall before he became ill.

℘

Lindsey got ready to leave her volunteer shift, her first one without her trainer being there. She recorded her hours in the ER volunteer notebook and looked up. Brady stood across the ER front desk from her. He watched her eyes light up. She recognized him, but it took her a second. His appearance differed, his hair and the uniform she decided.

She moved ahead toward him, stepping aside to let the ER staff by her. She left the crowded nurses station and walked toward Brady.

"It's so good to see you, what a surprise, Brady!"

"You really do volunteer here," Brady nodded his head as he smiled to her.

He followed her to the small locker area where Lindsey retrieved her coat.

"Uh, you didn't believe me when I told you?" Lindsey asked.

"To tell you the truth, I was skeptical, you, who tended flowers, a big step up, to these sick folks, but you're for reals, with your ER polo shirt and white slacks, you're the real deal."

She heard him, speaking to her with that same soft sincerity in his voice. They walked close together out into the large medical center parking lot.

Brady turned her to him, "I missed you."

Lindsey looked up to him, "And I have missed you."

Brady picked her up and walked around with her in a circle, "I have a couple of hours; can I see your dorm?"

"Yeah, let's drive there; you know the way, right?"

Brady nodded. He set her down, and they kissed.

Lindsey waited for him in the dorm lobby and walked him to her room.

He looked around at the neat, clean and organized room. "No roommate?"

Lindsey shook her head, "Supposed to have, but her parents came and got her stuff, lasted only one semester."

"School is definitely not for everyone."

Lindsey walked up to him, "That's for sure."

They kissed, warm feathery kisses, again and again. Brady picked her up and walked around in a circle with her. Lindsey felt an ache, slowly spreading from her groin up into her throat and the fire of it making her forehead sweat.

He set her down and took some deep breaths himself.

"You just do that to me Lindsey, set me on fire."

She gave him a sheepish smile and nodded.

"How about a late lunch, then I'll bring you back, plans tonight?"

Lindsey nodded her head again, "Tell you as we eat."

They sat across from each other at Hamburger Haven, a favorite joint for the younger college crowd who were not of drinking age. Plus it was close to campus.

"So, tell me about work, Brady."

"Periods of intense emotion, on the job, putting lives back together when we can, and then, the agony of what's next, what the next hope or tragedy will be. I'm not settling down very well to the down times. I spend time thinking about you. But I'll get more used to the hours, the stress. I work out, run, swim, when I'm off. So far, I'm not in my apartment very much, with the shifts so long, the weeks longer, and the time off all jammed together, always in the middle of the week, but I rarely have two days off together."

"That's 'cause you're low man, right."

"Uh huh, and I will be for a while."

"Is it pretty much what you expected?"

Brady looked into her eyes, "It is exactly what I expected; truly it's what I want to do, for some time to come. Every day is a medical adventure and I feel like I still have so much to learn, guess I never quit learning."

Lindsey smiled to him, "That's so great, so awesome."

"What about you, you haven't said much except about your classes, how much you like school, how it challenges you?"

"Yeah," she took his hand in her own, "Brady, I feel like I know where I'm headed, three years from now, my BSN, then test for my RN, that's it."

Lindsey stopped talking, waiting for him to say something.

"And?"

"And, you remember when you told me you wanted me to have a normal semester as a college kid?"

"I did."

"I'm having that now. I have a date tonight."

Somehow Brady knew those words would be coming. His gut felt like it got kicked by a big horse's hoof. But he plastered a smile on his face.

"Good for you, Lindsey."

"His name is Jacob, he's 19, he's in nursing like me, started a year ago last fall, had a kidney transplant that Christmas, and sat out a year. He's back; he says his life is a miracle and he's gonna give back."

"He appreciates his new life."

"Yeah Brady," she stopped and thought for a moment, "we have an expression that we say to each other a lot, me and Jacob, we're anxious to matter."

"When you're nurses, oh even before that, you'll matter, Lindsey."

She gave him a solemn thoughtful look, her eyes big and inquiring, "Do you think so, like, volunteering where I do, that I make a difference there?"

Lindsey nodded her head, affirming what she said.

She watched Brady's smile, "Yes, you do."

Back at the dorm Brady and Lindsey embraced as they stood by his SUV.

"Gotta get back; I am so glad I got to see you, Lindsey. I keep you in my thoughts and prayers."

"And I keep you in mine. I love you, Brady, think of you often; every time I hear an ambulance your determined face and quiet smile come to me."

"I love you, Lindsey, still serious as I tell you to have college experiences this semester. I want that for you."

She kissed him and let go, "Yeah, I'm younger than a lot of them and I need to feel what it's like to have fun as well as study.

℘

Spring break neared at IU. Jacob and Lindsey became close friends. They continued their breakfasts together and studied in the same location in the library at night. Lindsey kept her old habit of studying on the floor, spreading all her materials around her in an organized semicircle. All she needed was a solid chair to lean against.

Jacob encouraged her to attend church with him. That church's college youth group filled a very big room when they met. The youth group planned outings. A spring break trip took shape with the young people planning to help finish a church fellowship hall. A tornado destroyed the hall and took the roof off the church. The Iowa City church adopted the church in the town of Nearton, Arkansas after they learned what happened to the church. Members of the Iowa church started helping out. The Nearton church roof got replaced. A fellowship hall was next in the rebuild.

Jacob knew about Brady and Lindsey's relationship. Jacob had his eye on another woman in the nursing program. Lindsey knew about her. But he had a special tie to Lindsey.

Lindsey and Jacob worked side by side on the Nearton church. Together they painted inside the fellowship hall, which was much further along than the students expected when they first arrived. On the final day they got to work outside on the landscaping, planting trees and shrubs around the facility. It was on their last lunch of that final day Jacob decided to share. They sat on the ground with many of the youth group, in the hazy sunshine of that Arkansas day.

"Ya remember I told you I got my kidney a year ago at Christmas."

"Uh huh," Lindsey paused, she set her sandwich down, and turned her eyes to his, "yeah, go on."

"Pretty soon after we began studying together you finally shared with me that your mom died right before Christmas a year ago. And, and you told me because she was an organ donor, her organs got donated for transplants."

"Uh huh, did I tell you that I got to meet the woman who has mom's heart?"

"No, I didn't know that."

"Sheez, I cried so hard, the lady is alive today because of my mom. She was gonna, fer sure, die if she didn't get a transplant. She'd been on the list for a while."

Jacob touched Lindsey's shoulder and nodded, "I was too."

"What do you mean, Jacob?"

He saw her eyebrows raised in questioning.

"I was on a transplant list, for a kidney. Then I seemed to be doing so well that I came to IU a year ago last fall. My name stayed on the transplant list, and it was a good thing."

"Like you said when I met you Jacob, it's a miracle you're alive."

They finished their sandwiches and started in on their apples.

"So, Lindsey, when I told my folks about you and your circumstances, and what had happened to your mom my mom did some checking. And they finally heard back from the transplant folks. Mom and Dad are coming to see me Saturday afternoon and Sunday, to help make my spring break complete. They want to meet you."

"Sweet, I'd like to meet the parents of this special guy I am with all the time."

"But it's more than that, Lindsey."

They set their nearly eaten apples down. Jacob scooted closer to Lindsey and gathered her in his arms.

He whispered to her, "Lindsey, my replacement kidney is from your mom." Lindsey leaned back from him. Tears blasted her eyes as she tried to breathe and at the same time comprehend what he said. She put her hands to the sides of her face in disbelief.

"Oh, dear God, Jacob, oh dear God."

Lindsey cried and cried, wiping her face and nose on her dirty shorts. She came into his hug again.

"Mom, oh mom, I love you, thank you for what you continue to do for folks, Jacob, my friend, he has life because of you."

Now Jacob started to cry, "Lindsey, I've been given a second chance with my life."

They let go of each other.

"Jacob, how long have you known?"

"Just a couple of weeks, mom and dad, they want to meet you and learn about your mom. Do you have pictures?"

"Uh huh, two."

℘

"Unbelievable, unbelievable," Lindsey whispered to herself as she worked her shift in the ER on Saturday morning. The church group arrived back in Iowa from Arkansas early Saturday morning. Lindsey knew she was needed in the ER so she went in, tired but happy.

No matter what was going on in the ER, Lindsey had a chance to process everything that Jacob told her about his transplant. The ambulances kept coming in, one after another. All rooms had patients. As fast as Lindsey could clean and make a bed in the halls a new patient came to the bed. She peeked out in the emergency room reception area. Many people waited patiently in wheelchairs for an available ER bed. She looked in the wheelchair area. There were no more wheelchairs. Lindsey flew to the front of the hospital and wheeled two chairs back to the ER.

"Looks like it's not gonna settle down in here," she told herself.

But her shift neared its end. She decided to stay on a half hour longer. Lindsey kept praying for Jacob, that his health would remain good, with her mom's help. Lindsey recognized the face of a nurse who just came on the floor. He was from ICU. She felt good that ER borrowed more help.

"I gotta leave; I'm beat," she told the phone nurse at the front of the nurses' station who nodded and gave her a thumbs up.

"Jacob wasn't here in the ER last night, I sure can tell, with all the unemptied laundry bins and the cabinets lacking sheets and pillowcases, draw sheets and gowns. That was one of his big jobs, but Jacob and I were together last night, coming back to school."

ℰℴ

Lindsey found her favorite spot in the library Saturday afternoon and studied. She found Intro to Animal Biology to be her toughest class, she decided because it did not deal with humans directly. She grooved on Anatomy, the class she liked the most. She thought her other classes kind of fit in the middle. On her way back to the dorm she ran into two women from her floor who asked her to join them for an early dinner at Hamburger Haven.

Amber and Julie laughed with Lindsey as Lindsey explained the mess that happened to her during a cadaver demonstration in Anatomy.

"Actually, it was a liver; my lab mate turned wrong and it slipped off the table into my lap."

"Ooohhh, gross, slimy," Amber announced.

"Nah, actually the human body is a miraculous creation, so many intricate parts."

"You sound like a doctor, but you're doing nursing, right?"

"That's right."

ℰℴ

As Lindsey showered and got ready for bed that night, she remembered her commitment to Jacob and his folks. His parents wanted to meet her at a brunch after church.

She awoke from a sound sleep at 11:30 after falling asleep about 9. She heard a tap tapping on her door. Lindsey kept the guard on the door and opened it to see out.

"Jacob, what are you doing here?" she whispered.

"I wanted to see you; I miss you."

She closed the door and removed the guard. When she opened it again, he came into her room. It was dark except for the light shining from the nearly closed bathroom door. Lindsey's curtains remained partially open at night. She always wanted to look out at the moon and the stars.

"Do you feel what I feel for you, Lindsey?"

"How do you mean?"

"I want you in my arms and in my life; I got a second chance and I don't wanta screw it up."

"Jacob, you're my really good friend, the guy I tell everything to, the guy I trust. My world's been pretty tiny; you're helping open that world up to all kinds of possibilities."

They stepped closer to each other and they hugged. Jacob kissed her. She lifted her lips away from his and looked into his eyes.

"He cares," is what her eyes told her heart.

She kissed him back, kiss after kiss after kiss. Their hands went to each other's backs as they rubbed. Lindsey lifted his shirt and helped him take it off. He pulled off her pajama top. They held tight to each other. He stepped away from her, leaned and kissed each of her engorged nipples. She felt both the bulge of his erection and the moistness between her legs. They tossed off the rest of their clothes and lay together on Lindsey's bed.

Weeks before Lindsey and Jacob told each other of their one-time sexual encounters with someone else. The encounters were totally unsatisfying for each of them. The memory of that stayed in their minds. Their kissing and stroking heated to the point of complete wanting.

"Come with me on this journey, beautiful lady," he whispered to her.

"I am, I will," she spoke back to him as he entered her.

Later they lay locked together, kissing and speaking each other's names.

"This is the closest I've ever been to anyone, Jacob, to know you like this, to care for a friend like I care for you."

They separated a little as Jacob spoke, "My friend, I care, Lindsey."

They redressed in front of each other, an intimacy established between them. Jacob left after a half hour. They agreed to meet at the appointed place and time tomorrow for brunch.

Lindsey showered again, trying to examine in her head what had happened between Jacob and her. She couldn't. All she figured seemed that she did not feel for him what she felt for Brady. She loved Brady.

As she tried to go back to sleep at 2 a.m., she told herself it could not happen again with Jacob. He wore a condom for the sex they had. Lindsey did not want, under any circumstances, to get pregnant. She thought of the semesters ahead for her and of her relationship with Brady. She wanted him for her husband and the father of her children.

Jacob's parents pleased Lindsey a great deal. She liked them both. And she sensed the gratitude they had for Mariah, and the donated kidney for Jacob.

"Again, I'm blown away at what an influence my mom had on one single family, you folks," she nodded to them as she smiled.

Lindsey showed them the pictures of her mom and shared a bit of Mariah's life with them. Jacob heard much of the story from Lindsey when they first met, but he enjoyed being reminded of who this kidney donor really was, what her life was like.

As they all got ready to leave the restaurant, Jacob's mom spoke again,

"You are remarkable, Lindsey, picking up your life as a 16 year old, running what amounted to your mom's dream, then your dream. We will keep you in our thoughts and prayers, as we always do for Jacob. Your lives go on,"

she gazed from Lindsey to Jacob, "and from me and Jacob's dad, we want those to be good lives, filled with hope, promise, and love."

Jacob watched Lindsey start to cry as she heard his mom's words, "I still have a hard time when folks speak of mom," she paused and gulped for air, "for Mariah."

The four of them came together in a group hug.

"Time, it's the answer," Jacob's dad said.

Jacob walked Lindsey to her car, "Thank you for joining us; that's just about the most important conversation our family has had since my operation. We are all grateful, Lindsey. I hope we can continue to see one another."

They hugged, and Lindsey nodded up to him.

He turned and walked back to his parents' car.

ℰↄ

At breakfast Monday morning Lindsey ate with Jacob.

They spoke together in quiet tones.

"I value your friendship, Jacob. But sex will not be a part of our relationship. What happened Saturday night, exciting, but way out of character for me," she looked him in the eye, "you understand?"

Jacob nodded and beamed at her, "You are so desirable, but I understand there is another in your life."

Lindsey nodded back to him, "Yes, there is."

They agreed to have breakfast and dinner together in the dorm, but they began to go their separate ways in the evenings. Lindsey continued to spend her nights in the library, in her own special place where she could concentrate. Jacob no longer joined her there. At first Lindsey felt a pang of loneliness, but always she needed to concentrate on her school work.

ℰↄ

"I miss you like crazy, Lindsey. It's nuts here in Cedar Rapids, yeah, I got transferred, more pay, more hours, more responsibility, and I'm a little closer to you."

"Brady, that's so great, I miss you too. I got all A's, except for an A- in Biology."

"You are so smart; I knew you could do it, dear one, your summer plans?"

"I'm really happy to be living with Uncle Caleb and out of the dorm. I like being able to cook and bake; keeping house is a cinch in such a small place. Oh yeah, I'm taking Psych. Once that's done and I, of course, get my A, then I'm way sure I'll be in the School of Nursing, yeah my good grades. The class is a special 8-weeker this summer. I got a lot of time on my hands, so I took another shift volunteering in the ER, Monday morning, just two hours after my class, eeks that place takes a beating on Saturday nights and Sundays, people comin' in after Saturday night paaarrrtttiiees," she emphasized the word. "I try to help get things caught up. I swear, half the place is BH. Once they sleep off their drunken stupors and the rest of them get calmed down and get a med in them, well it's a fer sure more pleasant place."

"And?"

"Uh, so you think I'm doing more?"

"Yeah, right Lindsey," Brady paused, "remember I know you, what else?"

"Confess, something I love, I'm back in a busy florist shop, Tuesday through Friday afternoons for three hours a day. It's a blast, and it's so good to have my hands working and my nose smelling the flowers."

"So you study when?"

"At night, with just one class I plunk down on my bedroom floor, lean up against my bed with a pillow at my back, and you know my way, I spread all my stuff out in front of me in a semicircle so I can reach stuff."

"Yeah, I have an image of that in my mind. Will you ever study at a desk?"

"Nah, I can't concentrate; I know soon enough I'll have to be at a cubie or a station working on the computer. That's such a part of nursing now."

℘

Brady and Lindsey planned to be together for two days in August. Her class finished, and it was a few days before the start of fall classes. Brady had three days off together, the first time that happened. But before that Lindsey wanted to return to Porttown. Jen would be leaving for classes at Iowa State before long.

On her first afternoon back the two special friends took a picnic to a small lake where they fished and swam when they were younger. They swam with long lazy strokes out to the small pier in the middle of the lake. They sunned on the pier until more swimmers came along. Back they dove into the warm water and set a leisurely pace back to shoreline.

"This place holds such dear memories for me, Lindsey," Jen smiled to her as they sat eating the fried chicken Jen's mom cooked for them earlier in the day. They dipped carrot and celery sticks in the French onion dip Jen fixed. They polished the picnic off with the chocolate chip bars Lindsey made and brought with her for Jen and her family. At her uncle's insistence, she left a small plate of the bars for him.

"You can't leave until I see my plate of chippers," he declared as she got ready to visit Jen that morning. Lindsey watched his grin widen as he said that. She took the bars from their hiding place and pointed to them.

Jen laughed with Lindsey about having to hide the bars.

"What IS it about these chocolate chip bars, huh?" she asked Jen as they ate the last ones they brought to the lake.

"That's easy Lindsey, they're delicious and remind everyone of home, of mom baking cookies, back in the day."

Lindsey raised her eyes to the skies, a hazy blue that day.

She prayed, "Thank you God, for this wonderful day, for my friend, uh all my friends, for Brady. I am so blessed, I know it."

℘

Jen and Lindsey attended early mass the next day so Lindsey could head back to Iowa City. On the way home from church Jen drove to a coffee shop. They each ordered a large cinnamon roll, warm, with the frosting oozing into the roll and the extra melting down on the plate.

"You haven't talked much about your classes at IU, Lindsey."

"I've loved every minute, getting to know the human body, in Anatomy, and learning the basics of nursing in my intro class. Plus, volunteering in the ER, it's so real, the staff helping folks start to get well. What I like so much is having it thrust in my face, me, just a little volunteer, that it's all about the patient, totally and completely, moving the patient to health, whatever it takes."

"I know what you're gonna say next, so yes, I'll get into volunteering as soon as I can at school. Hey, how will I know if I really want to be a doctor unless I do that."

Jen watched Lindsey smile to her.

"So, Jen, what was I gonna say next?" Lindsey giggled to her as she drank the rest of her coffee.

"That," Jen paused, "it's best to be at a hospital or a clinic, that's where I'll be exposed most to patient care."

Lindsey nodded, "Yeah, at times you truly can read my mind."

"Subject change, what about Jacob?"

Lindsey now shook her head, "We made love, one time, it was right after we'd been away, spring break, for a week. We were together on the construction site and with each other all day and evening. We got so close; he knows my life story. But," Jen saw Lindsey's eyes darken from their usual green to gray, "I don't love him, Jen, I love Brady. And Jacob knows, it was a one and done. We are still friends and he is seeing someone."

"You gonna tell Brady?"

"Yes, I am, at some point, remember he told me to have a real college experience my first semester. And I have," she paused, "experienced so much since I got to IU, in the classroom, but also in the dorm and at the ER, and getting to know people, mostly older than me."

"I gotta get you back so you can head to school, sure hope you can come over to State to see me sometime."

"Same for you, Jen, I want you to come and stay with Uncle Caleb and me, once you feel comfortable at State."

Lindsey thanked Jen's parents for their hospitality and knowing that she always had a place in their Porttown home, her home away from home.

§⊃

Brady met her outside the ER on the Saturday he came to visit.

"How was your time?"

"Very interesting today, unbelievable, a patient, with a transplanted heart, what I didn't realize was how much medication she was on, all the meds she told the nurse for a variety of other things that were wrong with her, find it hard to believe she's still alive."

They walked along, hand in hand, as they left the hospital.

"As you well know," Lindsey turned and looked up into his face.

"Uh huh, the will to live is so strong in some folks. God's not ready to have them come home."

Lindsey caught his eyes and nodded, "Right, Brady."

He turned into her and leaned down to kiss her. She felt his lips, soft and warm, pressed to hers. They stood by his car, hugging each other.

"Dinner?"

"If it's OK, I'll fix us hamburgers and fries. Uncle Caleb is out with Lily. Uh, she's moved to Iowa City; working full time in a flower shop, also does wedding planning. They're so happy, Brady. She's taking two classes at the CC here."

"That's pretty wonderful for Caleb; school OK for him?"

"He's smart as heck; doing great, industrial engineering."

"Here's my address; wanta follow me?"

He nodded to her as she handed him the slip of paper with her address.

"I want to spend every minute I can with you, Lindsey, so can we stay in tonight after dinner?"

"That's what I want. Let's watch *Pearl Harbor*, have you seen it?"

Lindsey watched him shake his head, "I hear it's one heck of a love story."

She nodded to him.

"I'm staying with a friend, Lindsey. He's a paramedic, on duty tonight, how about let's go to church tomorrow and then we'll go out for the day, until I have to get back?"

Lindsey walked to him and they hugged, "Great, that'll be great."

Brady helped her fix dinner and set the table. They ate by candlelight.

"Lindsey, you know what?"

She eyed him, looking into his brown eyes, seeing a light in them, a reflection from the candles.

"What's that?"

"Dear one, this is the first meal we've had together, uh, in the place where you're living, the first one where it's just the two of us."

Lindsey's mouth was open to put in French fries. She closed her mouth and set her fork down.

"You're right." She touched his shoulder from across the table. "And I hope just the first of so many meals for so many years down the road."

Brady watched tears come to her eyes, "It's just that, good grief I'm 17, I have so much life to live. It's all been so jammed at me, until now."

"Until now," Brady paused, his eyes glimmering into hers, "that's why we'll do this one day at a time, each precious day," he paused again, "at a time."

Lindsey nodded and then touched her hand to her cheek, "I, I what I just said about all the meals, that sounded like I'm proposing to you."

She felt a red creeping from her neck up through her face, "Oh my gosh."

"Dear one, that's exactly what I heard, a proposal."

She looked across to him, "I love you, Brady, time isn't changing that."

He smiled and nodded to her. They watched the movie until the part where the pilot seemed to return from the dead. His lady was now dating his best friend.

"It's a love triangle; I'm not going to be able to stay to watch the rest, so tell me, Lindsey."

Lindsey explained the rest of the movie to Brady.

Brady stood to get ready to leave.

"Confession Brady, I just can't keep this from you. I had sex with a special boy, my best friend here at IU. It's over. It was a mistake."

She shook her head as her eyes teared, "I realize how much I love you, Brady."

He came to her and held her close. Brady stepped back from her.

"One night some months back two off-duty paramedics and I had way much to drink, a good time, chicks involved. I had sex, sheez," he stopped short and looked Lindsey in the eye, "used a condom, never saw her before or since. In the haze and the booze the whole deal, a one night hook up, mechanical, I don't even remember her name. That's so freakin' out of character for me. I disgusted myself," he shook his head. "I want you," Lindsey watched his eyes glimmer with passion into hers, "but someday, not now. I love you, Lindsey."

They came together and held on in a hug for a long time.

"Be safe, sweet wonderful Brady."

He whispered, "Dear one, my dear one."

7

During the last two weeks of Lindsey's summer she worked afternoons in the florist shop. She had delivery duty. It was her final Thursday, and she headed out soon after she got to work. The shop had a wedding delivery for a ceremony the next morning.

"I gotta get the van back to prepare for that," she thought as she walked up the steps of the beautiful home.

She held the birthday bouquet and rang the front doorbell. Lindsey noticed the closed screen door but the front door was open. She rang the doorbell again. She heard the tap tap of little footsteps on the hardwood floor coming toward her. A small dark-haired girl looked up to her from inside the door.

"Not s'posed to open the door for strangers, but you got flowers. Mommy," the wee one started to cry, "she fell from her chair, she's on the ground, she's hurt, can't talk."

"Sweetie, I'm comin' in; these flowers are for your mommy. Can you take me to her?"

Lindsey set the flowers down on the small table in the foyer. The little girl took her hand. They walked through the lovely home to the back patio. She saw a pretty mom lying on the ground, blood pooling from her head. What Lindsey noticed most was the purple look of the mother's face. She wasn't breathing.

"Sweetie, what were you and mommy having for lunch?"

"Hot dogs, curly fries with ketchup, I wuv ketchup."

"Did you eat all your hotdog?"

"Yes, mommy was eating hers, she stopped eating and pretty soon she fell off her chair."

Lindsey's mind peddled back as she thought about the times she hadn't completely chewed up a hot dog.

"Sweetie, grab your dolly that's in your chair and come and sit down, not too close to me, I gotta help your mommy."

Lindsey worked furiously to get the woman sitting upright and her body between Lindsey's legs.

"This better work, Lindsey, or you're gonna lose her," Lindsey muttered.

"Dear God, I wish I was a bigger person."

With all her might Lindsey did the Heimlich. It didn't work. Sweat poured from Lindsey's forehead as she moved the mother more upright. Lindsey placed her fist in position. With all her strength Lindsey did the press. The piece of hot dog flew out the mother's mouth as she started choking, trying to breathe. A few seconds passed as the mother regained the ability to breathe in and out. By now the flow of blood from the side of the mother's head lessened. Lindsey gently touched her head, felt the egg starting to rise where the mother landed after she fell from the chair.

"Sweetie, do you know where a phone is, please get it for me if you do."

The little girl knew exactly where to go, found the phone and brought it to Lindsey. With great care Lindsey eased herself from the woman and laid her on the concrete surface of the patio.

"Sweetie, what's your name?"

"Nicole."

"Do you know your address? I don't remember all the numbers, just the street name."

"What's your name?"

"Lindsey."

"My mommy and daddy and me live at 2265 Westwood Street."

"You're such a big helper, does your mommy tell you that?"

"Uh huh, a lot."

"I'm dialing 911; do you know about 911?"

"I do, I learned it at pre-school. I know how to punch it in, too."

Lindsey spoke to the 911 operator.

As soon as the ambulance arrived, so did the neighbors. They milled around outside until the ambulance got ready to leave. Lindsey gave her statements to the police. Nicole's mother began to talk in a low voice right before EMS lifted the gurney into the ambulance.

"Thank you, you, you saved my life," she whispered to Lindsey as Lindsey stood next to Megan's gurney.

Lindsey touched her shoulder, "I'm so glad I was delivering flowers to you from the shop where I work, Happy Birthday," she smiled to the woman.

Lindsey called the flower shop to explain why the van wasn't back. As soon as she returned to the shop they loaded the wedding flowers. Lindsey worked with the shop crew until 4:30. Lindsey looked over the flowers as she walked through the church and reception areas.

Out loud she said, "This may be the last wedding I ever work. What an experience it's been. Maybe someday I'll have a wedding of my own, someday."

Lindsey walked back into the church as they got ready to leave.

She looked over the beautiful setting and took a deep breath, "God," she prayed, "if it weren't for flowers, I doubt if I ever would've figured out what I really want to do. Thank you for guiding me."

ɕɔ

Lindsey had two messages on her landline in her apartment. One was from the assistant to the mayor of Iowa City. She offered Lindsey appreciation from the mayor for saving his daughter, Megan's, life. The mayor requested that Lindsey meet with him that evening. The location was his daughter's room at the hospital. Lindsey noted the time he asked her to be there. She took a quick shower and ate a PJ&B.

The entire hospital seemed so familiar to Lindsey now, like an old friend, from her time volunteering in ER. As she walked through the facility to the medical wing, that same warm feeling came to her. She recalled the warmth from when she turned 16, driving the van to the hospital in Porttown on Christmas Eve to deliver flowers. That hospital felt like a kind caring place, like this one she was in now.

She checked in at the nurses' station in the Med unit. The charge nurse smiled to her as she double checked the room number for Lindsey. The room door remained partially closed, so Lindsey knocked.

"Come in," she heard from a child's voice inside.

Lindsey opened the door wider and entered. The little girl, Nicole, came to her, took her hand and walked them both to the bed.

Lindsey gazed at Megan, then looked down to her daughter and touched the top of Nicole's head.

"You have a brave little daughter, Megan."

Megan smiled. Lindsey saw the bandage on the side of her head and her swollen face, cheekbone and bruised eye.

Lindsey heard clapping and thank you's from the group assembled in the room. For the first time Lindsey looked to the right and to the left. She saw a lot of people.

Once they stopped clapping, Megan took Lindsey's hand and squeezed it, "Thank you for saving me; you are sent from God. I believe that with all my heart."

Lindsey gazed at Megan.

"Well, God," she paused, "and the flowers, Megan, that led me to you. It was the flower delivery, your Happy Birthday flowers," Lindsey smiled to her.

Megan's father and husband came to Lindsey as she turned from the bed. They both shook her hand. Lindsey watched tears reflecting in both sets of eyes.

She heard "Thank you" from each of them.

"It's my birthday; staff said I could have a small bite of my cake, but I get lots of ice cream, that's better they said," as Megan began to laugh. "Lindsey, please stay and have birthday cake with us."

Jason, Megan's husband, served up the cake and ice cream. Nicole sat on the bed next to her mom as they ate their dessert. Everyone else stood as they ate cake and had punch. The mayor's assistant asked a few more questions of Lindsey, one being giving permission to publish a small story in the local newspaper.

೫೦

"Lindsey, I appreciate you inviting me to spend some of this weekend with you, now that finals are done."

She sat with her dad in the coffee shop where they agreed to meet after her volunteer shift in the ER. She still wore her green ER polo shirt and white slacks.

"As we met here in the entrance of the café I also noticed the green shoestrings in your white tennis shoes match the green in your shirt."

Lindsey laughed, "Dad, I've had a few comments about my green shoestrings."

"It's hard to believe your mom's been gone for two years."

"It's unbelievable, how time flies by. But mom goes on."

"I know, you wrote me," Lindsey's dad reached across the table to touch her upper shoulder, "about the woman who got Mariah's heart, and the nursing student, Jacob, who got her kidney."

"I wanted you to know, Dad, it helped me to work on my grief by writing you." She smiled to her dad, "I got lost in my anger, but it did no good. I need you, Dad," she nodded as he watched her eyes tear.

"And I need you, my daughter. You'll be 18 soon."

"Uncle Caleb will no longer be my guardian. Finally I'll be on my own, able to sign contracts, to have my own car insurance without him signing off."

"What're your plans?"

"Movin' out of Uncle Caleb's at the end of the December. Put a deposit down on a place, and then'll sign the rental agreement, by myself."

"Roommate?"

"Nah, not now, but maybe next summer or fall semester, depends, it's a two bedroom, furnished. I got pretty much nothin' in the way of furniture, some kitchen stuff, borrowing back some of what I lent to Uncle Caleb when he moved here, when we vacated the rental in Porttown."

"How's Brady?"

"Grand," she paused as he watched her nod and smile, "Dad, I love him very much. You get to finally meet him tomorrow; a rare Sunday off for him. He's driving here."

"What's different about your sophomore year in nursing, now that you've got another semester accomplished?"

"The nuts and bolts of what I'll do, Dad. Basic Care Concepts, 4 credits, Health Assessment, 4 credits, I love those two classes, oh and a nursing and society course, helps me understand how broad nursing is, out in the community at large. I kinda think only in terms of being in a hospital or a clinical setting. Nursing's so much more than that. Uh, this year is our backbone year, on which all the rest of my studies are dependent."

Joe O'Ranon nodded his head and smiled to Lindsey, "You already talk like a medical person, Lindsey. Did you hear yourself? You said this year of nursing is your backbone year."

"Wow, I guess that's true, did I really say backbone?"

"You did, you anatomy speak."

They laughed together.

"Dad, before we go, I got somethin' to show you."

Lindsey took a newspaper clipping from her coat pocket and laid it on the table for him to read. He read through it twice.

"My daughter," he teared up as he took one of her hands, "saved a life, that's wonderful," he paused as he looked at her, "awesome."

"I'm learning, enough now to benefit others, it's a way sweet feelin', Dad."

As she said that, her mind went directly to her mom, "See mom, what I'm doing, I know you are proud of me."

Lindsey's lips went into a big smile as she looked up and out to the other side of the restaurant.

"Talkin' to mom?" her dad asked as he watched her smile.

"Yeah, I was, I go to my quiet place."

ઈ౦

Lindsey went into her bedroom to change for going out to dinner with Brady and her dad. The men sat across from each other in the small living room of Lindsey's apartment.

Brady's brown eyes turned almost black as he smiled to Joe.

Joe watched him nod his head, "I am in love with Lindsey, and I am requesting your permission to marry her. We've asked each other to marry several times over the past two years. She is young, but wise beyond her years, thrust into the small business world when her mom died. She is very happy she is finally 18, so is her own boss."

Brady saw Joe smile across to him.

"I grant you permission. Lindsey's told me so much about you. Doggone it, I'll be tickled to have a son," he paused, "I mean, son-in-law."

"We're thinking Christmas of her junior year, a year from now. She's hell bent to get her nursing degree; she's got so much gumption, her grades are outstanding."

"Brady, how's that gonna work, you living in Cedar Rapids and her here at the University in Iowa City?"

"That's one of a number of concerns we have, and the fact that my hours change, there is not a definite routine for me, still low man in my group, so I get the difficult hours and two or three," he paused, "usually two different days of the week off."

"Won't that be hard because Lindsey will probably work 12 hour shifts, three days a week someday?"

"There's no doubt, Joe, the easiest times for us will be while she has the three semesters left of school after next Christmas. She'll have somewhat of a schedule with her classes, except for her practicum the next semester and her internship as a finishing senior."

Joe nodded his head to Brady, "Sounds like you two have worked through her remaining schedule, semester by semester."

"We have, it's so exciting for her, and I'm learning new stuff every single day as a paramedic. Coming up this summer I'll be doing some helicopter paramedic work."

Brady saw Joe's searching eyes, knowing what he might be thinking, "And yes, some of it will be Flight for Life."

℘

Brady arrived the next morning a little while before church. He hugged Lindsey, picked her up and walked around in a circle with her in his arms. When he set her down, she reached up and pulled his head down to kiss him.

"I love you Brady, did you sleep well?"

"Not, missin' you. Did your dad get off OK?"

"Yeah, he's very happy for us." Lindsey looked across the room and up, "Mom is too."

"I have to leave, from church, to head for my shift."

"So we'll take two cars."

The reverend delivered a Christmas message to the congregation. Brady and Lindsey held hands as often as they could during the church time.

"Hope, peace, love," what he said, Lindsey, special, for this special time of year."

He watched Lindsey nod.

"You're in my thoughts, Brady, always, and in my prayers," Lindsey said as she turned and looked up to him as they walked toward their cars.

"I want you to be as happy and truly blessed as your love has made me," Brady replied and squeezed her hand.

What he just said caused Lindsey to stumble. He caught her and helped her move forward in a more secure walk. She breathed in deep. They smiled to each other. Lindsey saw him off with a wave.

As she drove back to her apartment, she heard Brady's voice, his last statement to her, "Happy and truly blessed."

"I am, I really am," she heard herself whisper.

℘

Lindsey walked from the library in a haze. She just completed reading her assignment in her Psych-Mental health text.

"These folks will be the toughest for me to work with," she told herself, "honestly they scare the crap out of me."

Lindsey remembered her volunteering in the ER, something she gave up just a few days before. Some of the folks in the ER Behavioral Health unit showed up there because they stopped taking their meds. To her that was the biggest obstacle for a patient to overcome, understanding they were sick and needed their meds. Some mental health patients felt they didn't have a problem. But they kept returning to the ER.

"I'm so glad I had that volunteer experience," she nodded and looked up into the gray cloudy sky. She kept walking to her apartment near campus as she gazed around at the fall foliage, the reds and oranges and purple leaves.

"It's almost Halloween, happy times ahead," she spoke out.

ဆ

"So what do you think of your classes and being a junior?" Brady asked in his call to Lindsey.

"Right, we sure haven't talked about my classes, just our plans for Christmas, joining our lives together."

"Are you keeping the place with two bedrooms?"

"I am, it's older, but comfortable, a bedroom for us and a bedroom for guests, and a place for me to spread out on the floor to study. It's got new paint, carpet, new furnace and air, can live with the rest, has a dishwasher, only disadvantage is no washer and dryer."

"A central laundry area, don't think I even asked?"

"Uh huh, for the whole facility, yeah, classes, hard, my first practicum, the psych one, but I'm enjoying the parent child class."

"I get next Sunday off; my shift ends at 5 that morning. I want to be with you, Lindsey."

"I'll study like crazy all day Saturday so we can have Sunday together. When do you need to leave on Sunday afternoon?"

By 3:30, I got to get back and catch a little sleep before my shift starts Monday morning, at midnight."

"Precious hours, I will see you then, I love you, Brady."

"Back atcha, dear one."

They held hands through the church service, often gazing to each other.

"Let's do brunch and go back to my," Lindsey smiled, "I mean our place."

The noisy crowded restaurant kept their conversations to a minimum. They stood in the brunch buffet line twice.

"Well, I'm finally starting to fill up," Brady said as he dug into his second helping of scrambled eggs, bacon, sausage, fruit salad and two small cinnamon rolls."

"Me too, you have to eat when you can, Brady."

They washed their meal down with cup after cup of coffee.

"I gotta be alert as I drive back to Cedar Rapids."

Lindsey made coffee for them when they got back to the apartment.

They sat together, drinking their coffee and each holding the other's hand.

"Brady, I did it."

Brady paused, "Did what?"

Lindsey's green eyes pooled into his brown ones as she nodded her head.

"You did, you really did!" Brady spoke in a whisper when he really wanted to shout out.

They stood up, and Brady came around the table to her.

"It's time, Lindsey," she watched the brown of his eyes blacken as the passion rose in his eyes.

"Yeah, way past time," she smiled up to him.

He picked her up, walking around in a circle with her. He set her down and leaned down to kiss her. She returned his kisses with deep tongue kisses of her own. They held on to each other as they exited the kitchen. Brady removed her suit jacket and let it slip to the carpet. She kicked out of her heels as he pulled his shoes off. She removed his blazer jacket and laid it across the carpet floor. As they moved toward the bedroom they removed each other's clothes. They stopped often to kiss and caress each other.

At the bedroom door they stood naked together. Brady held her close, rubbing her back and pressing himself to her. Lindsey kneaded his buttocks and stepped away from him. She held his throbbing penis in her hands and stroked it. She continued to hold on to him as they approached the bed.

"I love you, Lindsey, my wife, the mother of my children."

"Soon, Brady, I love you."

They lay together, their breathing heightened and their touches more intense. Lindsey felt the moisture from her vagina between her legs and the ache in her whole groin area, a wanting ache.

They looked into each other's eyes.

"Lindsey?"

She nodded, "Brady."

He entered her, his ache matching hers. They stroked together, faster and faster until the explosion in her body zoomed to the top of her head. She felt his release of semen, his gift to her. They kissed, soft feather kisses, as he remained in her for a time.

They lay together on their backs, each touching the other's sweaty tummies. Lindsey came into his arms, on his right side, and put her arm across his chest. They dozed. Lindsey awoke in a startle reflex. She looked into Brady's open eyes.

"Hello, my love."

"I've imagined this time, with you, for so long, Lindsey."

They made love, again savoring every moment with each other.

"Our times together, they'll be so special, so sweet, Brady."

They showered together, exploring each other's bodies as they washed and rinsed each other. He wasn't hungry, so they sat with their coffee at the kitchen table.

"We actually never did get to finish our first cups," Lindsey laughed.

"We're doing it now. I gotta go. I love you, dear one. I want to thank you, helping me through the awful struggle of my job, the weird hours, the crazy times off. You been so patient with me for these two years, knowing that one day you'll have a schedule like I've got, you understand what I'm going through."

Lindsey stood by him at the front door, "I do understand, and for the sexual part of our lives, for you waiting so long for me, thank you, knowing how frightened a pregnancy would be for me."

He watched her smile, "It's so exciting, letting go, not worrying about a baby, birth control pills, our sex wonderful."

They held each other close. Lindsey looked up to him; she saw comfort in his eyes.

"I love you, Brady; you fulfill me."

He nodded and smiled as he walked out the door. Lindsey waited for him to turn back. When he did, she waved.

℘

"When do you want me there?" Jen asked.

"Just the day before the wedding, so the 27th, it's our tiny families for the rehearsal dinner, then the guys will go out, and you, me, Lily, and Brady's mom will go out for a pre-wedding girl time."

"Where are you now, Lindsey?"

"Out walking, are you done with finals?"

"Done, I'm headed for the seamstress to try on my maid of honor dress. It's a little large so she took it in on the sides. Lindsey, I'm so glad I'm wearing a black dress; it'll work for so many affairs that I'll need to attend in the future."

"Yeah, that's why my wedding dress is simple; the seamstress will whack off the bottom after the wedding so I can wear it as a regular dress. Jen, it's all such a dream, planning my wedding, so much fun. You and Lily helped me a lot, you with advice and Lily with everything else. Hey, you know she's a certified wedding planner now. She and Uncle Caleb, they're real happy, nuthin' official with them, I think Caleb wants the degree first and she's going to school too."

"How's Brady?"

"He's up in the heavens, for reals, he's doin' Flight for Life."

"Oh, Lindsey, oh my gosh, that's, wow, outstanding."

"Exactly what I said when he told me two weeks ago."

"When'll he move in?"

"Not for a while, until his new schedule gets stabilized. Jen, we knew it would be like this; we'll be together when we can. Health care, we gotta take our special times when we can get them."

"Christmas?"

"It'll be with Uncle Caleb and Lily, Brady's on duty. I will miss coming home to spend the holidays with you and your folks. Jen, I'm on the pill. Making love, wow, just wait, with the man you love, it's the most outa sight thing on the planet."

"Lindsey, that's so great; I can only hope for a guy like Brady, but that's so far down the road now for me."

"It'll come, with time, you got your path to walk, are you excited about med school?"

"Yeah, over the top, it's so far away. For reals, I got my MCAT guide book, studying it every chance I get, also take the practice exam as soon as I can. Plus I want to take a course, it costs but they prepare you for the exam. That just gets me to the beginning of med school. I gotta get accepted."

"You will be, our futures, oh Jen, everything is starting to come together."

"Fer sure, we'll talk soon, take care, Happy Holidays."

ℚ

"I'll pick up the church and reception flowers myself," Lindsey nodded to the florist shop owner, Sandy, for whom Lindsey worked during busy times.

"Does it seem strange to be working on your own wedding flowers, Lindsey?"

"Nah, working with flowers is just such a part of my world. I'm keeping it super simple in the chapel and in the room at St. Paul's student center. I've seen all the wedding extravaganzas."

She shook her head to Sandy, "Great for our business, but duh, for a couple of hours."

Sandy agreed, "Way past ridiculous, but that's what parents want for their daughters. And, sweet pea, we reap the benefits."

Lindsey smiled to her, "You are so right."

℘

"Sit down, Lindsey," is all she heard when she answered the phone. It was Darah McDern on the other line. Lindsey sat down on her bed.

"Darah, I just sat down, what's up, I know I'll see you tomorrow night."

"Honey, there's been an accident, the Flight for Life chopper, Brady was one of those on board, with an incoming patient."

A white flash whipped across her eyes, the same white flash she saw when she came upon the accident on that snowy country road several Christmas's ago.

"I'm in Cedar Rapids; Brady's got a broken leg and a really sore body. Somehow a wind shear caught the helicopter; it landed crazy. That's all I know. The pilot did not survive."

"Oh dear God, you're at the hospital?"

"Right, with Jared, he came with me."

"Brady's conscious, kinda in and out; none of the survivors are talking yet. Unbelievable, the patient they brought in was the least injured, well, on top of the condition that brought him in by Flight for Life."

Lindsey's mind swirled as her mental list took shape.

"I'm postponing the wedding; Brady must get well, first. I know he loves his flying duty; he'll want to get back to that after his recuperation."

"Thank you Lindsey, that's prudent of you."

"Would you like me to drive up to Cedar Rapids?"

"That would be wonderful; but, let me get the medical team's assessment in the morning and call you back. You're a medical person now. You know all this takes time."

"Darah, how are you doing?"

"Coping, keep us in your thoughts and prayers."

"I will."

"And Lindsey, I am praying for you. You're still coping with losing your mom. I'm praying for Brady and you, that your love will lead to your marriage. But I know now, it will be down the road. Please give all this time, Lindsey, that's what it will take, our patience."

"I agree. I'll look forward to your phone call."

𝕾

Lindsey ran to the kitchen with her cell. She made coffee, listened to the gurgles as it brewed, and drank a cup of the hot stuff mixed with a little water. At the same time she assembled her list of what she needed to do the next morning. Her first call was to Jen, her second to her dad, and the third to Uncle Caleb. She e-mailed as many of Brady and her close friends as she could. The rest she would call the next day.

Within an hour Uncle Caleb and Lily came and sat with her as she cried and talked and cried. They took over most of her list of phone calls that she needed to make the next day.

"He's in charge, you guys," Lindsey nodded her head as she saw them to her front door.

Lily hugged her, then Caleb hugged her and looked into her eyes, "Yes, Lindsey, God is in charge."

"Thanks for coming over and helping me tomorrow," Lindsey choked out as she began crying again.

Caleb touched the top of her head, "You be OK tonight, we can stay?"

"Thanks, but I need to be alone, my prayer," she stopped and breathed in, "soon, Brady and I'll be together."

They watched her tiny smile as she exhaled a deep breath.

𝕾

Lindsey started out soon after she got the call from Darah the next morning. She took her time on the highway to

Cedar Rapids. The road was plowed and sanded. Her mind whirled as she tried to concentrate on this day only.

"Tomorrow," she spoke out, "I will be with Brady, but not as part of a wedding ceremony. I have to do my part to help him get well."

She felt the tears well up in her eyes. For a second her mind crushed with disappointment until it came to her that this was a trial. But Brady lived, he was alive and she needed to celebrate that. He would become her husband, just not now, their love held them. Lindsey had a familiarity with the hospital in Cedar Rapids. She spent time there as part of one of her practicums.

The hospital front desk directed her to the orthopedic wing. She had his room number. A few feet from his door she stopped and put her back against the wall. She breathed in and out, counting to ten. It helped her relax.

"Smile, Lindsey, smile," she told herself as she entered.

"You're here, you're here, thank you God," she heard from Brady's hoarse voice directed to her.

He sat on the side of his bed. Lindsey did her quick nurse assessment of him. He sat up straight. She saw his left lower leg encased in a portable cast. Both of his legs were touching the floor, an orange booty on his right foot and a soft white sock under the cast for his left foot. Two crutches lay to the left of his leg. She glanced across to Darah and Jared and smiled. She directed her eyes to Brady's and tried to smile. What she saw was a haunted look in his eyes, a look she saw in many injured patients' eyes. He smiled and held out his arms to her. Lindsey moved in slow motion to his uninjured side. She leaned in and enclosed him with her arms. They held on to each other for several minutes.

"I love you, Lindsey, thanks for coming."

"I love you, Brady, I am with you, now and for all our tomorrows."

They continued to hold on in silence. When they released each other Lindsey gave him a soft kiss on his cheek. She did not want to disturb the stitches on his forehead and the small gash on his upper lip.

"Lindsey, God, He was with us, helped me to live, gave all of us life, except Tom, our pilot, oh dear God."

Lindsey heard sobs catch in his throat as he struggled to speak, "The medical team all survived, the best part, the patient is gonna make it."

"That's why you do what you do, to take the patient from health care to health."

Lindsey sat to his right on the bed as his mom and brother came around to be with them.

"So," Brady looked around at the three of them, "I got to get out and walk the floor. They'll let me out when they're sure I can handle my sticks. Want me to show you how it's going?"

They all nodded and watched him hop up with his crutches and start to walk out.

"See, they already fixed me up with foam for under my arms; that's what gets chafed so fast with the walking."

"Brady, what about your concussion; your mom told me you were unconscious last night."

"Came out of it around 2 a.m.; CAT scan done, no indication of swelling, hematoma, or worse."

Lindsey walked to the left of Brady, just in case he weakened. His mom and brother walked ahead of them, turning often to watch his progress. He walked at a slow pace, trying to get comfortable with his left leg just up off the floor.

"So, bro, when you gonna blow this pop stand?" Jared asked.

"Tomorrow, I'll convalesce at my place for several days, then it's back to work, I'll be on dispatch, wanta get back to work as soon as I can."

Lindsey looked to Brady, "When will you be able to put weight on your leg?"

"A few days, after they do an X-ray to see how the bone's healing; it was a simple break, God sure blessed me with this one," he nodded to Lindsey.

"Time to get back, Brady, you're slowing down, and the little aches are getting bigger."

They settled Brady in his room and he started to doze off.

"I need coffee, can I buy you two a cup in the cafeteria?"

They sat around a small round table in the quiet hospital cafeteria.

"Lindsey, this's gotta be a tough situation for you; your wedding was tomorrow. I appreciate you not mentioning it to Brady."

"Right, Darah, we will get married," she smiled as she touched Darah's shoulder. "I'm thinking sometime in the spring, maybe IU's spring break in early April. What do you think about that?"

Darah nodded, "But it's you and Brady's deal."

Jared watched his mom and Lindsey as they talked.

"They'll do so good together," he thought, "she's exactly the daughter that mom never had, so knowing exactly what mom wants, and how to go about getting it. Hey, I'm a little bit in love with Lindsey myself."

The three of them returned to Brady's room. They waited until Brady roused.

"Bro, we gotta head back. You'll be fine; we had to see for ourselves."

"You and mom, you'll get my car from my duty station and take it to my apartment, right?"

Jared replied, "Dude, that's what we agreed. The station will give me the car keys?"

"Yeah, they know. I gave them my locker combination so they'll get in to retrieve my keys. You've got my apartment key, so when you get the car there, just leave the keys on the kitchen counter."

"Got it," Jared smiled to his brother.

Darah and her son said their goodbyes and left Brady and Lindsey.

Lindsey crawled up into bed with him and snuggled into his neck. They remained silent as they both drifted off for a little while. Lindsey's exhaustion caught up with her. She hardly slept the night before, for worry of Brady. A nurse woke them with pain meds for Brady. They went for a short walk and returned for Brady's dinner. Lindsey asked, and dining services brought her a dinner too. They ate together, savoring every bite. Brady was hungry, and so was Lindsey.

"That tasted so wonderful; glad you got your appetite back," Lindsey smiled to him as they ate.

They talked about Lindsey staying at Brady's place for the night. She had a key to his apartment and had visited him there once.

"It's been over 24 hours since the accident; I need to go, Brady, I bet they release you soon."

"Go, dear one, take a long hot shower for me, gonna insist on a shower in the morning, whether I leave or not, I got to get clean. Being sick is smelly, gross, especially after that accident."

Lindsey sat next to him on his bed. She looked into his eyes. Then she took her hands and gently started at the top of his head and slipped her hands down his face and then his shoulders and his arms. She kissed him.

He watched her smile to him as she nodded and said, "You, you, are God's masterpiece."

Brady tried to smile, but the pain medicine started taking hold of him. He closed his eyes. Lindsey kissed the top of his head and left the room. She hurried from the hospital to his apartment. She felt exhaustion take hold of her, like a whirling wind carrying her away. She lay down on Brady's bed and went to sleep.

She awoke at 4 a.m. and showered. Lindsey found his coffee pot in the lower cupboard where he kept it. She made a full pot and drank most of it.

"I'll have breakfast with him in his room. Maybe they'll release him sometime today."

As she sat at his apartment table two images came to her, the last time she saw her mom, and kissing Brady goodbye last night. Tears filled her eyes as she cried and cried.

"God help me, I'm selfish, but today, it, it was to be my wedding day. Mom, you didn't get to see it, but maybe you will, one day."

Just then the tears came hard, choking her, making her scream out, "Why, why Lord."

She put her head in her hands.

She shook her head as she spoke out, "Wrong, that's wrong, what, it's what, do I do now, Lord?"

Her tears continued, again to the point of the phlegm choking her throat. She felt like she was losing control of herself, an insurmountable grief pulling her.

She screamed out, "God, help me hang in there, to help Brady, to get him back to work, until he can go back out on regular duty."

Lindsey put her head down on the table and breathed, in and out, like she told the patients she worked with to do. The breathing calmed them down, and did the same for her.

ℰↄ

At the Ortho nurses' station she asked for a breakfast to be sent up for her in Brady's room. Brady's door was partially closed. She knocked and heard his voice, "Enter."

She suspected, from the tone of the voice she heard, he knew it was her.

Brady saw her smile, her real smile, her eyes shining, the woman he loved, right here in front of him. She came to him and kissed him on the lips.

"I was careful, Brady, to kiss just that one section of your lips, I see the gash, like I know you feel it."

"Chow coming?"

"Right, I ordered a breakfast for me, too."

She watched his smile spread across his face.

"Hey, I'm 99% sure they'll release me today. Got up early and took a shower. Tomorrow's the pilot's funeral. I gotta go to that. Then I want to go back on duty. My supervisor will decide and let me know today. I'm so excited about returning."

"Hey, slow down slick, how did you sleep last night?"

"Good, it was the meds, what about you?"

Lindsey nodded her head, "Exhaustion, I just landed on your bed with all my clothes on, I was out," she smiled and nodded.

"That's real good. I want you to head back today. Christmas came and went. This accident has made some changes in our lives, Lindsey."

"Yes, it has," she smiled to him. "Hey, Brady, what about driving?"

"I knew you were going to ask me that, sure as heck glad that I have automatic transmission in my SUV. Since it's my left leg, I'm cool to drive and brake with my right."

Staff brought their breakfasts. They both cleaned up their plates; Brady asked for a half slice of Lindsey's toast.

"Coffee's pretty good here."

Brady smiled to her, "Yeah, it better be, this was the most expensive breakfast so far in my life."

Lindsey shook her head, "What?" she thought for a moment and said, "Oh yeah, the cost of a hospital stay, even just one day."

Brady's Ortho doc arrived a half hour later. He released Brady after Brady showed him how well he got around on his crutches. Brady also agreed to do several sessions of physical therapy. Lindsey carried the hospital discharge sack as they entered Brady's apartment.

"How about some coffee; I'll be back, I must change out of this scrub outfit; they gave me this when they had to cut my uniform and flight suit off me."

Lindsey made another pot of coffee and found a partially open sack of chocolate chip cookies in the pantry. They sat together in the silence. Brady began to cry. Lindsey watched the tears glistening in his eyes and falling on his cheeks.

"Give me your hand, Lindsey, we have to talk."

She nodded to him as she felt the pressure of his hand over hers.

"When the wind shear hit us, I thought we would all die. The last thing I said when we slammed into the ground was to God. It told him I was ready, to go with Him, to go to heaven. Then I blacked out. When I woke up, there, in that hospital room, I was oozy for a little bit, but then my head cleared. It came to me, that I'm not ready to marry you, Lindsey. You're still very young. I need time out, and your studies are so critical. I want you to concentrate everything into your school work. I gotta try to figure out where I'm headed, figure out if what I'm doing is just too doggone dangerous. I love my work, but right now I have fear, about everything in my life. Please, please, can you possibly understand?"

"I do, Brady, I do. Time, we gotta have time; we're in God's hands."

"I get that, and it's God's time, He'll let us know when it's our time to be together. Dear one, I'm so tired, so mixed up. Right now I don't know my purpose, why I'm on this earth."

Brady hung his head over the table and started to cry again.

"Let's get you to bed, Brady. Then I'll head back."

She helped him to his bedroom and helped him take off his shirt and shorts and walking cast with his crutches nearby. His crying lessened. Lindsey kissed his forehead.

"Your meds, if you need any, are on the kitchen counter. Brady, please listen to me."

Brady opened his eyes as he lay there. She saw the black of his enlarged pupils and the veined red everywhere else in his eyes.

"Brady, you have purpose, it will come back to you. I feel helpless, but I do not judge you, you have to do what you feel is best for you. I will pray and pray, and time, that's what we need. I dedicate my semester to you, to do the very best I can. I love you."

She kissed him on the forehead and watched as he closed his eyes. She saw his lips, a tiny smile on them. She felt tears gush from her eyes as she removed the engagement ring he gave her. Lindsey set it next to his meds on the kitchen counter.

8

Lindsey held her emotions in check on the way back to Iowa City. She picked up her mail and stepped into her apartment. She took her bag and mail to her bedroom and knelt by her bed.

She whispered, "God, help me get through this time. I thought I would be married and on my way to our honeymoon suite by now. Let it go, Lindsey, the disappointment will smack you around for a long time. What did Brady say to me?" she thought back to their talk at his kitchen table a few hours ago, "'concentrate everything on your studies.' Well, God, that much I can do. I'll go back to the ER, maybe get my Saturday volunteer shift back. God, bless and keep my Brady."

She called and left a voice mail for Uncle Caleb. She asked him not to call her, that she was shutting her phone off until the next day, she needed to sleep.

❧

It turned out Lindsey felt she had a fine spring semester of her junior year. She worked with the elderly as part of her gerontological nursing. Lindsey never was around grandparents or people that age. She enjoyed their wisdom and sense of humor. From watching her WWII movies for all those years she understood older folks and their patriotism, their love for their fellow soldiers, having each other's backs.

In her public health nursing class she found where she might belong when she finished, out with the public, not in a clinic or hospital. She even considered that working with a nonprofit might be her purpose in nursing. Lindsey saw herself in all sorts of scenarios playing out, maybe a visiting nurse working in an area where health issues dominated poor people's lives.

Jacob and Lindsey returned to their friendship. He listened to her as she cried through her explaining Brady's accident. Jacob assured her that a time away might be a good thing for Lindsey, to find out what she wanted for her life, where she might want to be without Brady.

"I'm here for you, Lindsey," his eyes bored into hers as she nodded.

Stats turned out to be a more fun class than either Lindsey or Jacob expected. Neither one of them thought much about the numbers in health care, what percentage of folks would have Alzheimer's, what probabilities and possibilities existed for folks with serious heart conditions. They wrestled with the stats on diabetes and obesity and how those diseases affected patients.

ᔕᗞ

The summer before her senior year she worked almost full time in the flower shop where she helped part time during breaks from school. Lindsey caught the eye of a newly completed medical student, now an intern in one of the facilities where Lindsey would have a practicum in the fall. They went on several dates and saw each other occasionally during her fall semester. Lindsey felt no spark for him; she knew he was looking for a wife, preferably a nurse. At Halloween she ended it. Brady continued to stay on her mind. He became like a dream to her, a dream she had often at night. Most of the time in her dreams she saw him standing in the ER. He smiled, waiting for her to finish her volunteer shift. Brady and Lindsey called each other almost every month to stay up with each other's lives. He knew she made a serious commitment to a job in the tri-state area where Tennessee, Georgia and North Carolina met. The nursing position would be with a non-profit, working with impoverished folks with health issues, especially in Tennessee.

Lindsey had no interest in the money. All through her IU semesters she lived frugally, paying for her tuition and everything else connected with going to school. She had a tidy nest egg saved for a home someday, for her kids' college funds someday. Lindsey wanted to help in an area where patients needed an enormous amount of health care. That was in the Appalachian South. In her last semester before her BSN, she planned to register for her boards in both Iowa and Tennessee the same month she would graduate.

Each night before she went to bed, before she brushed her teeth she stood at the bathroom mirror and spoke out, "God, I love Brady, I don't know when or if we will ever make a decision to join our lives together. But I have to go on, to do what I'm passionate about, health care for folks."

※

Her final semester at IU came. Besides her internship at a community hospital outside of Iowa City, she still went to campus on Monday mornings for her Nursing Leadership Care Management and Contemporary Issues classes.

"Switch, Lindsey," she told herself as she sat on the floor in her bedroom with her books around her in a semicircle, "time to study for boards."

She maintained her five hour a night schedule of studying she kept through her whole nursing curriculum. Lindsey found that difficult on nights when her internship kept her until 9 p.m.

She often shook her head, laughing, "This semester, geez, it reminded me of when I turned 16, after mom died, studying for my GED plus studying for the ACT and SAT. "

ℰ♄

Billy D. nearly caused her to break down, something she felt confident she never would do as a medical person. She thought she saw it all as a volunteer in the ER in Iowa City. Now she was in a different medical setting, at a community hospital, and she was finishing her internship. Billy D. came in twice, from falling. From the ER he got moved, once to the pediatric wing and the second time to orthopedics.

When she saw him in Ortho, she knew. She felt the flip flop of her stomach and a knot of pain exploding in her head. The pain was her anger. Lindsey gained his confidence when he was patient in Peds. This time, in Ortho, Billy D. told her the whole falling story, two falls. She wrote out her statement of what he told her and gave it to the police officer who her supervisor called. X-rays explained a lot that Billy D. blocked out of his mind forever. He was seven years old, and his bones showed the extent of his abuse.

"Nurse O'Ranon, you gonna help me?" Billy D. asked her once the room quieted from other medical personnel leaving.

Big tears showed in his eyes as she touched his good shoulder.

"I am, Billy D., you're gonna go to folks who'll take good care of you."

"Thank you for listening to me."

Lindsey looked him in his teary eyes, "God bless and keep you, Billy D."

He left the hospital three days later, with another family. Lindsey got a chance to meet them. Her mind gave her good vibes for this family and for Billy D. These relatives talked in a serious manner about caring for him. Lindsey learned the man and woman he lived with, the abusers, his uncle and aunt, would spend a long period in prison.

℘

Over spring break Lindsey visited the medical personnel at the nonprofit in Tennessee. The folks the nonprofit helped lived in a corner of Tennessee that bordered Georgia and North Carolina. They joked that their sort of well-known area was called the Little Frog Mountain Wilderness area. Lindsey laughed harder when they explained with very serious faces that they were not far from the Big Frog Mountain Wilderness area.

"Well, I definitely must see these locations if I move here," she told the staff who interviewed and spent time with her. When she got the news that the job was hers, she made her commitment to move to Ducktown. She would begin her work for the nonprofit as soon as she completed her RN requirements.

℘

"This your last volunteer week, Lindsey?" one of the ER nurses asked her as she finished making the bed. A man sat in the wheelchair close to the bed.

Lindsey raised a finger, "One more, then graduation," she signaled to the nurse who stood nearby.

"Your bed's all ready for you, sir," she smiled to man. She saw the IV dripping into his arm.

"Thank you, young lady," she heard the hoarseness in his voice. He tried to smile. From her experience and the vital signs she saw as she looked at the patient, she felt her nurse feel. He was very sick.

Her morning volunteer shift ended, and she filled in her hours in the notebook. It was the same white notebook from these past four years. She put the notebook back on the lower shelf. Brady stood on the other side of the nurses' station, smiling to her, as he had the first time he came to the ER to see her after her shift.

Lindsey looked out to make sure she erased her name from the white board that indicated who was on shift. Brady watched her turn her eyes from the board to him. At first she did not recognize him. She saw his closed-cropped dark hair and the weight loss in his face. He watched tears pool in her eyes as she stood there with her mouth half open. She moved through the break in the counter around the station and walked to him. Lindsey reached up as he reached down to hug her. They held on, for a long time.

"Let's go to the cafeteria, OK?"

She nodded her head, looking to him, still not sure it was Brady.

"It's been so long, thank you God," Lindsey raised her head above and ahead as her mind raced back to those many months ago, when the helicopter crash occurred.

They held hands as they walked along, keeping their eyes on each other. Lindsey and Brady found an empty table in a quieter area of the hospital cafeteria.

"Coffee?"

"Yeah, thanks Brady."

He got them each a cup; they both drank it black.

"You're more beautiful now, wow, than I remember you at 16." He looked down at her white tennis shoes and smiled up to her, "You've still got your green shoe laces."

They laughed together about the shoe laces and Lindsey's keeping those same shoes for so long.

"My handsome man," Lindsey smiled as she nodded to him.

He took her hand and held it, "I'll love you forever, for all my life, and then with God in heaven," Brady said as his brown eyes smiled into hers.

"Brady, I've prayed for this day, this special wonderful day. I love you; I never gave up on you. I just knew one day." Brady watched as Lindsey stopped and took in a deep breath, "That this day would come."

They talked for a time, cried together and smiled and held hands.

"I'm wanting to take a paramedic position in your area of Tennessee. It's available in July. I drove down, interviewed; incredible the needs; we have so much here, we are so blessed. What I saw, it was like being in a third world country."

Lindsey nodded to him, "It pretty much is like that there. It took some initiative for you to make your decision. I'm awed that you want to, to work in an area with impoverished folks."

"I want to be with you, Lindsey, wherever you are."

He took her hand again.

"Marry me, share your life with me, loving, giving, caring."

From his shirt pocket he took the engagement ring she gave back to him after his accident.

"Wear my ring, I love you, Lindsey."

She looked across to him as she watched his eyes light up. She nodded, "Yes, yes I will marry you."

Brady slid the ring on her finger. As Lindsey felt the tiny weight on her finger, she felt a large burden of doubt and sadness lift from her mind. They watched the tears come to each other's eyes. They held hands, both their hands as their emotions cascaded into more tears.

"Let me take you out to dinner, an early one, 'cause I have to be back to Cedar Rapids by 9 p.m. My shift starts at 11."

"OK, I'll study hard tomorrow and tomorrow night. My internship requires lots of paperwork, so that's part of my studying. Let's go for a walk. It looks like rain later."

They held hands as they walked and talked for several hours. Lindsey and Brady stopped at a park bench.

"I know you are crazy busy; I took the time to talk to the pastor at St. Paul's. I'm being bold, but I did it anyhow. He could marry us, Lindsey. He gave me two early Friday evening dates soon after you graduate. His Saturdays at the chapel are all booked for weddings, way into July."

Lindsey nodded her head. He watched her raise her eyes to him, "I appreciate you checking. I would just want your mom and bro, my dad, Uncle Caleb and Lily and two of my nurse friends, one guy and one gal, and a couple of your friends. Perfect, what made you think of all this?"

"Like I said, you have to take care of business, remember, it's what I told you the last time we were together, when I asked for a time out. I'm perfectly capable of doing a wedding. Just tell me about flowers and catering."

They stood up and hugged.

"Sandra still has a record of our flower order on the shop's computer; you know where I've been helping out. For a late wedding dinner let's do it where ever you can get reservations, maybe with a room for a group our size. What cha think?"

"Perfect, you make it all sound so doable."

"I want simple, it's about you and me and folks we love," Lindsey looked up at him as she took his hand, to walk for a little longer.

They strolled the park path, watching the squirrels zooming along tree branches and the bloom on the spring lilacs. They held each other's hands, stopping again and kissing. Lindsey felt the soft ply of his lips on hers. She lifted her eyes to his caring face.

"I doubt if I'll sleep tonight; so much has happened in the last couple of hours."

Brady smiled to her, "Yeah, you will, dear one, I'm with you, hold on, you're in my arms, for now, and soon in Tennessee."

JUST LET IT GO

14-year-old sophomore Saralita Gonsalves copes with her new school and community in Georgia. Grandma Tami becomes her legal guardian when Sara's mom goes to prison. After a church service fellow calculus student, Evan, recognizes Sara. He exchanges greetings with them and says he will see Sara at football practice. Sara manages equipment for the Hillyer Hawks football team.

Evan and Sara become friends. They share their love of football, interest in aeronautics, and that neither one lives with their parents. Sara protects herself after an assault by a football player. Walking from mass Tami gets shot in the shoulder, and a bullet grazes Sara's head. The police determine the shooter's motive to be retaliation against Sara's mom.

At the holidays Sara participates with the football team in a visit to a senior living facility and dances at a Ball. Her Christmas present is a visit to Family Space Camp during spring break, with Evan, his uncle and her grandma.

Missing her mother catapaults Sara into a mental meltdown. With Evan's help and counseling she begins to understand her being scared about everything that's happened to her.

Sara gains the friendship of Marissa and Madala. She runs cross country and sings in a choir her second semester at Hillyer. Evan wants her to see other guys. She dates Gadan while Evan is away for the summer. Her Columbian biological dad writes to Sara. She begins to communicate with this man she has never known.

During her second fall semester Sara decides on being just friends with Evan. They visit the universities they have talked and dreamed about for so long, Georgia Tech for Sara, and Cal Tech for Evan. Sara appreciates the strong grandma she's come to know and love. At a Christmas brunch Evan and Sara share how much they mean to each other. Evan helps her understand how far she's come.

ABOUT CATHLEEN

www.CathleenEllis.com

Cathleen Ellis is a Colorado native. She and her husband, John, live in the northern part of the state. They have four sons, three daughters-in-law, and four grandchildren. Cathleen draws the inspiration for her love stories from the lives of young people with whom she has lived and worked her entire life.

www.ingramcontent.com/pod-product-compliance
Lightning Source LLC
Chambersburg PA
CBHW020012140726
47904CB00018B/2230